倍斯特出版事業有限公司
Best Publishing Ltd.

我的第一本萬用親子英語

陳怡歆、洪婉婷 ◎ 著

MP3

教小朋友說英文
不要再只會It is an apple. My name is Tom.

這本書讓你成為寶貝最棒的英文老師！

- 用**52個情境式小對話**，在家輕鬆打造全英文的**地理課、自然課、生物課、化學課**和**歷史課**！

- 由**兩大親子主題**組成——**學校課程**和**親子教育**，從各類基礎課程、親子溝通到家庭教育。
  以簡單小對話開始，學會**主題字彙、熟背慣用語**，再進階到說出一個**完整句子**，
  有效地循序漸進學習，是一本適合親子一起學習共同成長的英語學習書。

Preface
作者序

　　說到學英文，台灣人雖普遍有「英文很重要」的觀念，但分數至上的填鴨式教學，往往讓快樂的學習成了許多孩子的夢魘。以前常有人問我怎麼愉快地學英文？我想，最基本的還是要與生活結合。英文應該活用於生活中，而非為了應付考試。因此，我在撰寫此書時秉持著三項原則，也可說是本書的三個特色：**一、趣味性：**學英文一定要有趣，因此，我盡量以輕鬆、日常的口吻撰寫對話，就像平日談話一樣自然。**二、連貫性：**每個單元的對話、例句盡可能撰寫成類似短篇故事般的連貫內容，這樣讀起來會更有全面性的圖畫，而非單獨零落的片段。**三、道地風味：**收錄道地美式用語，讓學片語不再只有 not only but also，而是有更多活潑生動的美式俚語，讓你一開口就讓人驚艷！

　　許多人在小孩即將出生或出生後，除了喜悅之外，內心或多或少對他們的未來有著種種的規劃，比方說：構思著如何教育孩子，希望孩子在幼稚園或小學就讀雙語學校，讓孩子英語能力早早贏在起跑點。

　　其實比起分數，培養孩子學習英語的「興趣」和「學習動機」是更重要的。在最初的學習階段，不該是用背了多少字彙和分數，去衡量孩子的英語學習情況。**《我的第一本萬用親子英語》**規劃各種不同的主題，父母親可藉由本書，了解孩子們喜歡的類別，並且鼓勵他們學習相關的主題，養成學習英語的動機。

　　每一次的學習都在建立孩子的學習信心，偶爾也跟孩子一起唸錯，讓孩子了解學習就是別怕犯錯，這只是學習的一個過程，自然就不會排斥學英語。企盼藉由本書，讓親子互動更親密，父母親與自己的寶貝一同快樂學習、快樂成長。

編輯部 敬上

Instructions
說明頁

水族館校外教學 ❶
~~eld Trip to the A~~

🎙 **情境對話**　💿 MP3 001

- Ms. Lin 林老師
- Students chant 同學們歡呼
- Smarty Sophie 聰明的蘇菲

M: Hi class. We are here at the Monterey Bay Aquarium today. Are you excited?

S: WE LOVE THE OCEAN! WE LOVE AQUARIUM!

M: Can anyone tell me what is the largest animal in the ocean?

S: I know! I know! It is the blue whale.

M: You are correct! A blue whale can grow up to 30 meters in ~~ngth~~ and more than 180 ~~s~~ in weight.

林： 嗨，全班。我們今天在蒙特利灣水族館。你們興奮嗎？

同： 我們愛海洋！我們愛水族館！

林： 誰可以告訴我，海裡最大的動物是什麼？

聰： 我知道！我知道！是藍鯨。

林： 你答對了！藍鯨可以長到 30 ~~長~~，體~~18~~

從一分鐘小對話開始，家長和小朋友輪流扮演不同角色，互動式學習激發小孩的創意。

中英文左右對照，學習更 easy！

延伸學習字彙
- quiet 　　安靜的
- fierce 　　凶狠的
- scary 　　嚇人的
- fluffy 　　毛茸茸的
- cuddly 　　討人喜歡的
- bouncy 　　活蹦亂跳的

Cat

認識動物
- golden retriever 黃金獵犬
- Persian 　　波斯貓
- macaw 　　金剛鸚鵡
- goldfish 　　金魚
- rabbit 　　兔子
- hamster 　　倉~~鼠~~

~~olden retriever~~

唸完短對話後，家長可以先請小朋友指出可能出現的單字，培養主動學習的習慣，一鼓作氣認識更多單字。

慣用語 MP3 002

keep an eye on 留意

❶ **Keep an eye on** the dolphins while watching the performance.
在看表演時，注意看海豚。

❷ Teachers always **keep an eye on** their students to keep them from danger.
老師們總是留意他們的學生使他們遠離危險。

慣用語和延伸句型都標上
不同顏色，閱讀起來清楚
明瞭，也讓學習更有重點。

bring back 帶回

What did you **bring back** from your
你從旅途中帶了什麼

 延伸句型 MP3 003

❶ can anyone 誰能告訴我

Can anyone tell me what is the largest animal in the ocean?
誰可以告訴我海中最大的動物是什麼？

❷ it is 這是

It is the blue whale.
是藍鯨。

❸ grow up to 生長到

超值 MP3
家長與孩子一起聽、一起讀，
聽力和口說一起練起來！

005

Contents
目次

Part 1

贏在起跑點－課堂知多少

進入校園，小朋友在學校有更多機會接觸不同領域的知識，這時候他們就像一塊海綿，充滿好奇心，也是培養閱讀和主動學習的最好時機，為往後的學習之路打下良好基礎。

用親子最熟悉的主題，讓你跟孩子一起開口大聲練習英文，贏在起跑點！

Field Trip to the Aquarium ❶
水族館校外教學 ❶

 情境對話   MP3 001

- Ms. Lin 林老師
- Students chant 同學們歡呼
- Smarty Sophie 聰明的蘇菲

M: Hi class. We are here at the Monterey Bay Aquarium today. Are you excited?

S: WE LOVE THE OCEAN! WE LOVE AQUARIUM!

M: Can anyone tell me what is the largest animal in the ocean?

S: I know! I know! It is the blue whale.

M: You are correct! A blue whale can grow up to 30 meters in length and more than 180 metric tons in weight.

S: Wow!

林：嗨，全班。我們今天在蒙特利灣水族館。你們興奮嗎？

同：我們愛海洋！我們愛水族館！

林：誰可以告訴我，海裡最大的動物是什麼？

聰：我知道！我知道！是藍鯨。

林：你答對了！藍鯨可以長到 30 公尺長，體重超過 180 公噸。

同：哇嗚！

1 贏在起跑點—課堂知多少。

2 伴著孩子成長—親子教育。

Aquarium

延伸學習字彙

· excited	興奮的
· largest	最大的
· correct	正確的
· fearless	無懼的
· coward	膽小的
· tiny	小小的

Blue whale

認識海底世界

· aquarium	水族館
· blue whale	藍鯨
· dolphin	海豚
· sea lion	海獅
· shark	鯊魚
· wale shark	鯨鯊

  MP3 002

keep an eye on 留意

❶ **Keep an eye on** the dolphins while watching the performance.

在看表演時，注意看海豚。

❷ Teachers always **keep an eye on** their students to keep them from danger.

老師們總是留意他們的學生使他們遠離危險。

. . . .

bring back 帶回

❶ What did you **bring back** from your vacation?

你由假期中帶回了什麼？

❷ Please **bring back** the books you borrowed from the library as soon as possible.

請盡快將你在圖書館借的書歸還。

 延伸句型　　MP3 003

❶ can anyone　誰能告訴我

Can anyone tell me what is the largest animal in the ocean?

誰可以告訴我海中最大的動物是什麼？

. . . .

❷ it is　這是

It is the blue whale.

是藍鯨。

. . . .

❸ grow up to　生長到

A blue whale can **grow up to** 30 meters in length and more than 180 metric tons in weight.

藍鯨可以長到 30 公尺長，體重超過 180 公噸。

（側欄）

1 贏在起跑點——課堂知多少。

2 伴著孩子成長——親子教育。

Field Trip to the Aquarium ❷
水族館校外教學 ❷

 情境對話  MP3 004

・Ms. Lin 林老師
・Hip Hop JC 嘻哈傑西
・Sporty Jimmy 運動健將傑米

M: Now who can tell me what kind of fish is Nemo from the cartoon "Finding Nemo?"

林：現在有誰可以告訴我卡通『海底總動員』中的『尼莫』是什麼魚？

H: It's the clownfish. They are usually yellow or orange with white bars, and they live with sea anemones.

嘻：是小丑魚。他們通常是黃色或橘色，且有著白色的條紋。他們與海葵住在一起。

M: Great job! I wonder why they live with sea anemones. Does anyone know?

林：非常好！我在想他們為什麼與海葵住在一起。有人知道嗎？

S: It is because the sea anemones protect clownfish from being eaten by other bigger fish.

運：這是因為海葵可以保護小丑魚免於被其它比他大的魚吃掉。

M: I am so impressed. Now let's go into the aquarium and explore even more.

林：我實在是太驕傲了。現在讓我們到水族館做更多探索。

1
贏在起跑點——
課堂知多少。

2
伴著孩子成長——
親子教育。

Clownfish

延伸學習字彙

- usually　　通常
- wonder　　想，懷疑
- protect　　保護
- impressed　驕傲的
- explore　　探索

Sea anemone

認識海底世界：

- clownfish　　小丑魚
- sea anemone　海葵
- sea star　　　海星
- coral　　　　珊瑚
- sea turtle　　海龜
- mambo fish　曼波魚

be able to　可以，有能力

❶ She **is able to** speak 5 different languages.
她能說五種不同的語言。

❷ Kids **are able to** bring candies on Friday.
孩子們星期五可以帶糖果。

once again　再一次

❶ Girls asked their mother to tell the story **once again**.
女孩們要求他們的媽媽再說一次故事。

❷ Boys got onto the roller coaster **once again**.
男孩們又再一次上了雲霄飛車。

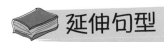 延伸句型　 MP3 006

❶ usually　通常

They are **usually** yellow or orange with white bars, and they live with sea anemones.

他們通常是黃色或橘色及有著白色的線條，並與海葵同住。

❷ I wonder　我在想

I wonder why they live with sea anemones.

我在想他們為什麼與海葵住在一起。

❸ let's　讓我們

Now **let's** go into the aquarium and explore even more.

現在讓我們到水族館做更多探索。

Unit 03 — The African Theme Party
非洲主題派對

 情境對話　 MP3 007

- Ms. Lin 林老師
- Elegant Mary 優雅瑪莉
- Hip Hop JC 嘻哈傑西
- Big Tom　大湯姆

M: Look at your hand-made costumes. Who wants to tell me what JC is?

E: From the beautiful spots on his face and body, I think he is a cheetah.

H: Yes, I am. I'm also the fastest running mammal on land.

M: Fantastic! Tommy, can you introduce yourself?

B: I am a rhino. People are trying to hunt me down for my horn.

M: That's very cruel. Don't worry, we'll protect you.

林：看看你們的手工變裝服。有誰可以告訴我 JC 是什麼？

優：從他臉上及身上的美麗斑點可以看出，他是獵豹。

嘻：是的，我是獵豹。我也是陸地上跑最快的哺乳類動物。

林：太棒了！湯米，你可以自我介紹嗎？

大：我是一隻犀牛。人們為了我的角而企圖獵殺我。

林：這件事實在非常殘酷。不用擔心，我們都會保護你。

1 贏在起跑點——課堂知多少。

2 伴著孩子成長——親子教育。

Rhino

延伸學習字彙

- hand-made   手工的
- beautiful   美麗的
- fantastic   極好的
- cruel   殘酷的
- protect   保護

Cheetah

認識非洲：

- rhino   犀牛
- cheetah   獵豹
- tiger   老虎
- lion   獅子
- hippopotamus   河馬
- zebra   斑馬

 慣用語  MP3 008

differ from　不同於

❶ **Differ from** his brothers, he prefers reading than playing sports.

不同於他的兄弟，他喜歡閱讀勝過運動。

❷ Students are not allowed to have school bags **differ from** the ones that school provides.

同學不可以帶學校發放以外的書包。

....

don't worry　不要擔心

❶ As long as you did your best, **don't worry** about the result.

只要你盡你所能，別擔心結果。

❷ **Don't worry** about the traffic. We will be on time.

別擔心塞車。我們會準時的。

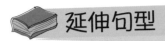 延伸句型　 MP3 009

❶ from 從

From the beautiful spots on his face and body, he is a cheetah.

從他臉上及身上的美麗斑點可以看出，他是獵豹。

❷ introduce 介紹

Tommy, can you **introduce** yourself?

湯米，你可以自我介紹嗎？

❸ hunt … down 打獵

People are trying to **hunt me down** for my horn.

人們為了我的角而企圖獵殺我。

Unit 04

Jurassic Park ❶
侏羅紀公園 ❶

- Ms. Lin 林老師
- JC 傑西
- Smarty Sophie 聰明的蘇菲
- Tommy 湯米

M: Hi, class. Today, we will discuss about Jurassic Park. What's your favorite dinosaur?

林：嗨，同學好。今天我們要來討論侏羅紀公園。你們最喜歡的恐龍是什麼？

S: My favorite is diplodocus. It had a long neck that it would have used to reach high and low vegetation, and to drink water.

聰：我最喜歡的是梁龍。因為牠有長脖子讓它能觸及高處和低處植物和用於飲水用途。

JC: Tyrannosaurus is the coolest. It is one of the most fearsome animals of all time. Its bite was around 3 times more powerful than that of a lion.

傑：暴龍最酷了。牠是史上最可怕的動物之一。牠的咬力是獅子的三倍強勁。

M: Marvelous! Could dinosaurs fly?

林：優秀啊！恐龍會飛嗎？

T: Not really. Pterosaurs were a relative of the dinosaur that could fly. They were known as the flying reptiles.

湯：不會。翼手龍是恐龍的親戚，牠會飛。牠們是會飛的爬蟲類。

1 贏在起跑點──課堂知多少。

2 伴著孩子成長──親子教育。

Tyrannosaurus

延伸學習字彙

- favorite　　最喜歡的
- vegetation　植被
- coolest　　 最酷的
- fearsome　　可怕的
- powerful　　強勁的

Pterosaurs

認識恐龍：

- dinosaur　　 恐龍
- tyrannosaurus　暴龍
- pterosaurs　　翼手龍
- diplodocus　　梁龍
- triceratops　　三角龍

off all time 歷來的

❶ Stephen Curry is one of the best basketball players **of all time**.

史蒂芬‧柯瑞是歷來最好的籃球選手之一。

❷ Superman is the strongest hero **of all time**.

超人是歷來最強壯的英雄。

known as 作為…而知道

❶ The bakery is **known as** the best store in town.

這間麵包店被認為是城內最好的商店。

❷ Italy is **known as** the country of pizza.

義大利被認為是比薩之國。

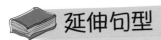 延伸句型　 MP3 012

❶ discuss about 討論有關於

Today, we will **discuss about** Jurassic Park.
今天我們將討論關於侏儸紀公園。

❷ one of the …的其中之一

It is **one of the** most fearsome animals of all time.
牠是史上最可怕的動物之一。

❸ relative of 親戚，親屬

Pterosaurs were a **relative of** the dinosaur that could fly.
恐龍的近親中會飛翔的是翼手龍。

1 贏在起跑點──課堂知多少。

2 伴著孩子成長──親子教育。

Unit 05

Jurassic Park ❷
侏羅紀公園 ❷

 情境對話　 MP3 013

· Ms. Lin 林老師
· Ron 榮恩
· Kelly 凱莉

M: Jurassic Park is a well-known film about dinosaurs. Who has never watched or heard of this movie?

R: My brother and I have watched it over 100 times.

M: Great! In fact, these gigantic creatures are ancestors of birds, can you imagine?

K: Then how come they don't have feathers?

M: It's a matter of evolution. Somehow after millions of years, dinosaurs became all kinds of flying birds.

林：《侏儸紀公園》是一部著名有關於恐龍的電影。有人從來沒看過或是沒聽過這部電影嗎？

榮：我跟弟弟已經看過一百次了。

林：很好！其實這些巨大的生物是鳥類的祖先，你們能想像嗎？

凱：那為什麼牠們沒有羽毛？

林：因為演化的緣故。經過數百萬年，恐龍就成了各種在空中飛翔的鳥類。

K: Wow! That's incredible.

凱：哇！真是不可思議。

Evolution

延伸學習字彙

· avian	鳥類的
· fossil	化石的
· reptile	爬蟲類的
· dominant	優勢的
· terrestrial	陸地上的
· cold-blooded	冷血的

Stegosaurus

認識恐龍：

· pterodactyl	翼龍
· brontosaurus	雷龍
· velociraptor	迅猛龍
· oviraptor	偷蛋龍
· stegosaurus	劍龍

how come　為什麼

❶ It's already November. **How come** it's still so hot?
已經十一月了。怎麼還是這麼熱？

❷ **How come** there are no kids playing trick or treat this year on Halloween?
為什麼今年萬聖節沒有孩子上門要糖果？

....

somehow　不知怎麼地

❶ **Somehow** the climate is getting more and more bizarre.
不知道氣候怎麼越來越奇怪了。

❷ The news of Jake and Amy broke up **somehow** spreads out in the campus.
傑克和艾咪分手的消息不知怎麼在校園裡傳開了。

 延伸句型　🔊 MP3 015

❶ have / has never done something　從沒做過某事

I **have never** stayed home alone overnight.
我從來沒有自己一個人在家過夜。

....

❷ in fact　事實上

In fact, whenever I have to stay home alone, I go over
to my friend's place.
事實上，每次我得一個人在家時，我都會到朋友家去。

....

❸ it's a matter of　是⋯的問題；是因為⋯的緣故

It's a matter of courage. I just can't stand to be around
with nobody.
這是膽量問題，我就是不敢自己獨處。

1
贏在起跑點──
課堂知多少。

2
伴著孩子成長──
親子教育。

Unit 06

Rainforest
雨林

 情境對話　 MP3 016

- Ms. Lin 林老師
- Jimmy 傑米
- Patty 派蒂

M: We have two different types of rainforests, temperate and tropical rainforests.

J: How come there is so much life in the rainforest?

M: Warm and rainy weather helps plants grow; therefore, animals would have plenty of foods to eat. Brightly colored birds and tree frogs are the typical rainforest animals.

P: Are the rainforests in danger?

M: Yes, they are. People in many areas are cutting down trees. We must tell them that this will

林：我們有兩種不同類型的雨林，溫帶雨林與熱帶雨林。

傑：為什麼有這麼多生命在雨林裡生活？

林：溫熱且常下雨的天氣幫助植物生長。因此，動物有很多食物可以吃。顏色亮麗的鳥類及樹蛙便是典型的雨林動物。

派：雨林現在處於危險中嗎？

林：是的，他們是危險的。許多從各個不同區域的人在砍

affect our lives.

樹。我們必須告訴他們，這會影響我們的生活。

1
贏在起跑點──
課堂知多少。

2
伴著孩子成長──
親子教育。

Tropical rainforests

延伸學習字彙

- different   不同的
- rainy   常下雨的
- therefore   因此
- plenty   許多
- brightly   顏色亮麗的

Tree frog

認識雨林：

- tropical   熱帶的
- tree frog   樹蛙
- toucan   巨嘴鳥
- caiman   凱門鱷
- orangutan   猩猩
- temperate   溫帶的

 慣用語 MP3 017

how come 為什麼

① **How come** dad got two scoops of ice-cream, but I only got one?

為何爸爸有兩球冰淇淋但我只有一球？

② **How come** you are always late to school?

為什麼你總是上學遲到？

....

therefore 因此

① He did not finish his homework last night; **therefore**, he was punished to clean the bathroom.

他昨晚沒有完成他的作業，因此他被罰掃廁所。

② She was talking on the phone while driving; **therefore**, she got a ticket from the police.

她邊講電話邊開車，因此被警察開了一張罰單。

延伸句型  MP3 018

❶ different types of 不同類型的

We have two **different types of** rainforests, Temperate and Tropical rainforests.
我們有兩種度同類型的雨林，溫帶雨林與熱帶雨林。

・・

❷ how come 為什麼

How come there is so much life in the rainforest?
為什麼有這麼多生命在雨林裡生活？

・・

❸ therefore 因此

Warm and rainy weather helps plants grow. **Therefore**, animals have plenty to eat.
溫熱且常下雨的天氣可以幫助植物生長。因此，動物有很多食物可以吃。

Unit 07

Globe and Map
地球儀和地圖

 情境對話　 MP3 019

- Ms. Lin 林老師
- Jenny 珍妮
- Ashely 艾許莉
- Tony 湯尼

J: Ms.Lin, what is the difference between a globe and a map?

A: I know! A globe is a small model of earth, whereas a map is a representation of a location.

M: Well done! Does anyone know other facts about a globe and a map?

T: Maps are usually flat. There can be many kinds of maps, such as a map of the school, or a map of a city.

珍：林老師，請問地球儀和地圖有什麼不同？

艾：我知道！地球儀是地球的小模型，而地圖是表示某一個地區。

林：非常好！還有沒有人知道其它關於地球儀和地圖的事實？

湯：地圖通常是平面的。地圖有很多種類，例如：一個學校的地圖，也可以是一個城市的地圖。

M: You guys pretty much answered Jenny's question. Great job!

林：你們幾乎已經回答了珍妮的問題。做得好！

1
贏在起跑點——
課堂知多少。

2
伴著孩子成長——
親子教育。

Globe

延伸學習字彙

· between	之間
· representation	代表
· location	地區
· fact	事實
· flat	平面的

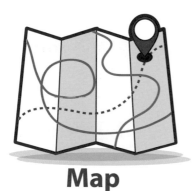

Map

認識地圖：

· map	地圖
· treasure map	藏寶圖
· climate map	氣候圖
· road map	路線圖
· topographic map	地形圖
· physical map	自然地理圖

 慣用語  MP3 020

the difference between 與…之間的不同

❶ We are twins. Sometimes even our parents cannot tell **the difference between** the two of us.
我們是雙胞胎。有時甚至我爸媽無法說出我們兩個之間的不同。

❷ Can you tell **the difference between** a poodle and a beagle?
你可以說出貴賓狗與小獵犬之間的差別嗎？

pretty much 幾乎

❶ He **pretty much** got the perfect score this time.
他這次幾乎滿分。

❷ She is so poor that she **pretty much** eats nothing every day.
她如此窮以至於她每天幾乎都沒有吃東西。

延伸句型　MP3 021

❶ whereas 然而 / 卻…

A globe is a small model of earth, **whereas** a map is a representation of a location.

地球儀是地球的小模型，而地圖是表示某一個地區。

1 贏在起跑點 —— 課堂知多少。

2 伴著孩子成長 —— 親子教育。

❷ other facts about 關於…的其他事實

Does anyone know **other facts about** a globe and a map?

有沒有人知道其他關於地球儀和地圖的事實？

❸ such as 例如

There can be many kinds of maps, **such as** a map of the school, or a map of a city.

地圖有很多種類，例如：一個學校的地圖也可以是一個城市的地圖。

Sculpture
雕像

 情境對話　 MP3 022

• Ms. Lin 林老師
• George 喬治
• Amber 安貝兒

M: Hi class. We are going to make sculptures today.

G: What is a sculpture?

M: A sculpture is a three-dimensional art. For example, the Statue of Liberty is one of the famous sculptures.

A: Sounds like fun. Although, I don't know where to start.

M: In tradition, stone, wood or clay is the usual materials. Nowadays, people use all kinds of things. So, use your imagination.

林：嗨，同學好。今天，我們要來做雕像。

喬：雕像是什麼呢？

林：雕像是一個立體的藝術品。例如，自由女神就是一個有名的雕像之一。

安：聽起來很有趣。儘管我不知道要從何下手。

林：傳統上來說，石頭、木頭或泥土是一般的材料。現今，人們使用各種材料。所以，運用你的想像力吧。

A: I got so many ideas and can't wait to start.

安：我有好多想法而且等不及要開始了。

The Statue of Liberty

延伸學習字彙

- three-dimensional　　立體的
- famous　　有名的
- although　　雖然
- tradition　　傳統
- nowadays　　如今

Sculpture

認識雕像：

- The Statue of Liberty
  自由女神 （美國，法國）
- The Great Sphinx
  獅身人面像 （埃及）
- Manneken Pis
  尿尿小童 （比利時）
- Christ the Redeemer
  救世基督像 （巴西）
- Abraham Lincoln Statue
  林肯雕像 （美國）

慣用語

 MP3 023

be going to 即將

❶ The new pet store **is going to** start the babysitting service next month.

新開的寵物店將在下個月開始提供保母服務。

❷ Because of his bad behavior today, he **is going to** detention this weekend.

因為他今天不好的行為，他將在這個週末留校察看。

although 雖然

❶ **Although** she was sick for the past few days, she still maintains her perfect score.

雖然她過去前幾天都生病，她還是維持她完美的成績。

❷ **Although** he did not win the prize, he is still grateful that he joined the event.

雖然他沒有贏得獎品，他還是很慶幸他參加了這個活動。

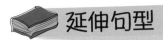 延伸句型  MP3 024

❶ for example 例如

For example, the Statue of Liberty is one of the famous sculptures.
例如，自由女神就是一個有名的雕像之一。

❷ in tradition 在傳統上來說

In tradition, stone, wood or clay are the usual materials.
傳統上來說，石頭、木頭或泥土是一般的材料。

❸ can't wait to 等不及

I got so many ideas and **can't wait to** start.
我有好多想法且等不及要開始了。

Unit 09 **Frigid Zone**
寒帶地區

 情境對話 MP3 025

- Ms. Lin 林老師
- Joseph 喬瑟夫
- Peter 彼得
- Tony 湯尼

M: Frigid zone is also called the polar region.

J: Do people live in the frigid zone?

M: Indeed! But very little. This area is created from ice.

P: I also heard that during winter, it has a complete darkness. During summer, you can have 20 hours of daylight.

M: Very good! The temperature can be as low as -68 degree Celsius.

T: I wonder if there are any living creatures.

林：寒帶地區又稱做極圈區域。

喬：有人住在寒帶地區嗎？

林：當然！但很少。這個區域完全是由冰造的。

彼：我聽說在冬天時，天完全是黑的。在夏天，卻可以有20小時的白天。

林：非常好！氣溫也可以低到只有攝氏－68度。

湯：我想知道這區有沒有任何生物。

M: You can find blue whales and penguins in the Arctic Ocean.

林：你可以在北冰洋找到藍鯨及企鵝。

Polar bear

延伸學習字彙

· polar	極圈
· indeed	確實
· complete	完全的
· tradition	傳統
· living	活的

Frigid zone

認識極圈動物：

· polar bear	北極熊
· penguin	企鵝
· walrus	海象
· seal	海豹
· muskox	麝牛
· wolf	狼

 慣用語  MP3 026

indeed 確實

❶ As a student representative, Joe is **indeed** the most popular student in school.

身為學生代表，喬確實是學校最受歡迎的學生。

❷ Blue whales **indeed** are the biggest creature in the ocean.

藍鯨確實是海裡最大的生物。

---

as···as 與···一樣

❶ Jennifer is **as gossip as** her mother.

珍妮佛和她媽媽一樣八卦。

❷ To follow his father's footstep, he works **as hard as** his father.

為跟隨他父親的腳步，他和他爸爸一樣認真工作。

 延伸句型　 MP3 027

❶ be also called　也稱作是

Frigid zone **is also called** the polar region.
寒帶地區又稱做極圈區域。

❷ during　期間

During summer, you can have 20 hours of daylight.
在夏天，卻可以有 20 小時的白天。

❸ wonder if　想知道是否

I **wonder if** there's any living creatures.
我想知道這區有沒有任何生物。

Temperate Climate
溫帶氣候

 情境對話 MP3 028

- Ms. Lin 林老師
- John 約翰
- Patty 派蒂

J: Don't we have the best weather or what!

M: I can't agree with you more. Average yearly temperatures in a temperate climate are neither burning hot nor freezing cold.

P: Which cities have the temperate climate?

M: Places like London, the weather can be unpredictable. One day it may be sunny, the next may be rainy. Places like San Francisco on the other hand, have a dry summer. With all that said, most places with a temperate climate have

約：我們真是擁有最好的氣候啊！

林：我完全同意你的看法。溫帶氣候的平均年氣溫既不會太熱也不會太冷。

派：哪些城市擁有溫帶氣候呢？

林：地方像是倫敦，天氣可能難預測。一天可能是晴天，隔天可能下雨。在另一方面，地方像是舊金山，就有乾燥的夏天。說了這麼多，大部分溫帶氣

four seasons.

候的地方都有四季之分。

Pear

延伸學習字彙

- agree　　　　　同意
- burning　　　　炙熱的
- freezing　　　　結冰的
- unpredictable　不可預測的
- season　　　　季節

Temperate Climate

認識極圈水果：

- pear　　　　梨子
- pome　　　　梨果
- plum　　　　李子
- grape　　　　葡萄
- kiwifruit　　　奇異果
- apricot　　　杏子

neither…nor　不是………也不是

❶ She is **neither** angry **nor** upset about her daughter's behavior.

關於她女兒的行為，她既不生氣也不難過。

❷ The weather today is **neither** too hot **nor** too cold.

今天的天氣既不會太熱也不會太冷。

on the other hand　另一方面

❶ John is good at public speaking, **on the other hand**, his brother is good with writing.

約翰擅長公開演講，另一方面，他弟弟則擅長寫作。

❷ My sister loves to stay home and read, **on the other hand**, she enjoys hanging out with friends, too.

我姊姊很愛待在家讀書，另一方面也喜歡和朋友們聚會。

  MP3 030

❶ don't …or what! 還真是…啊

Don't we have the best weather **or what**!
我們真是擁有最好的氣候啊。

❷ agree with 同意（與某人意見相同）

I can't **agree with** you more.
我不能同意你更多。

❸ with all that said 說了這麼多

With all that said, most places with a temperate climate have four seasons.
說了這麼多，大部分溫帶氣候的地方都有四季之分。

1
贏在起跑點——
課堂知多少。

2
伴著孩子成長——
親子教育。

Unit 11

Atom and Molecule
分子與原子

 情境對話    MP3 031

- Ms. Lin 林老師
- Jason 傑森
- Betty 貝蒂
- Anthony 安東尼

J: Ms.Lin, what is water made from?

M: Has anyone ever heard of H2O? Before we define H2O, we should know two words: Atom and Molecule.

B: Atom is the basic object that occupies space. It can be solid, liquid, or gas.

A: When two or more atoms combine, they give rise to a molecule.

M: Very good. Now H2O is a molecule where two hydrogen atoms combine with one

傑：林老師，請問水是什麼做的？

林：有人聽過 H2O 嗎？在我們定義 H2O 之前，我們應該要知道兩個字：分子與原子。

貝：分子是充斥在空間裡最小的東西。它可以是固體、液體或空氣。

安：當兩個以上的分子結合時，他們會成為一個原子。

林：非常好。H2O 就是一個結合了兩個氫分子與一個氧分

oxygen atom also called water.　　　子 的 原 子 也 稱 為
水 。

1
贏在起跑點——
課堂知多少。

2
伴著孩子成長——
親子教育。

Oxygen

延伸學習字彙

· atom	分子
· molecule	原子
· define	敘述，説明
· basic	基礎的
· occupy	填滿
· combine	結合

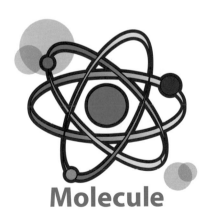

Molecule

認識分子：

· oxygen	氧氣
· solid	固體
· liquid	液體
· gas	氣體
· hydrogen	氫氣
· carbon	炭

慣用語

 MP3 032

either…or… 是…或…

❸ You can **either** take the bus **or** ride a bike.

你可以坐公車或騎腳踏車。

❹ He is going to pick **either** chocolate **or** strawberry ice-cream.

他將會選巧克力或草莓冰淇淋。

....

combine… with 結合

❸ When you **combine** ice-cream **with** milk, you create milk shake.

當你結合冰淇淋與牛奶，你製作了奶昔。

❹ His job is to **combine** singers **with** the world-class bands.

他的工作是結合歌手與世界級的樂團。

 延伸句型　　MP3 033

❶ made from　製成

Ms.Lin, what is water **made from**?

林老師，請問水是什麼做的？

❷ have ever　曾經有過

Has anyone **ever** heard of H2O?.

有人聽過 H2O 嗎？

❸ give rise to　產生 / 引起

When two or more atoms combine, they **give rise to** a molecule.

當兩個以上的分子結合時，他們會成為一個原子。

Unit 12

Solar System
太陽系

 情境對話　 MP3 034

- Ms. Lin 林老師
- Kimberley 金百麗
- Ray 雷
- Class 同學

M: Hi class. Today we are going to learn about the Solar System.

林：嗨，同學，今天我們要來認識太陽系。

K: I know! There are nine planets in the Solar System !

金：我知道！太陽系有九大行星。

M: That's correct. Who can tell me which one is the closest to the Earth?

林：沒錯。誰能告訴我最靠近地球的是什麼行星？

Ray: I think it's Mercury.

雷：我認為應該是水星。

M: Actually, that's the closest planet to the Sun. Your assignment today is to find out the array of the nine major planets in the Solar System.

林：實際上，那是最靠近太陽的行星。你們今天的作業就是找出太陽系中，九大行星的排列順序。

C: Not again!

同：不是吧，又有作業了！

1 贏在起跑點——課堂知多少。

2 伴著孩子成長——親子教育。

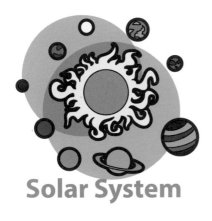

Solar System

延伸學習字彙

- ecliptic　　黃道的
- vast　　　浩瀚的
- infinite　　無限的
- solar　　　太陽的；太陽能的
- universal　宇宙的；世界性的
- gravitational
　重力的；引力的

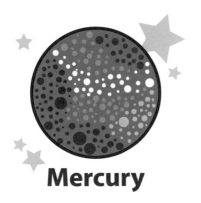

Mercury

認識行星

- Mercury　水星
- Venus　　金星
- Mars　　火星
- Earth　　地球
- Jupiter　木星
- Saturn　土星

that's correct / that's right　沒錯

❶ Son: Dad, do I really have to finish dinner to have a blueberry pie?

Father: **That's right**.

兒子：爸爸，我一定得吃完晚餐才能吃藍莓派嗎？

父親：沒錯。

❷ Buyer: I'd like to return this oversized jacket. Should I just put it back in the case and bring my receipt?

Clerk: **That's correct**.

顧客：我想退還這件過大的夾克，是不是放回盒子裡，再附上收據即可？

店員：沒錯。

not again　又來了；真討厭

❶ Kim: Remember to bring your umbrella! It's raining.

Donna: **Not again**.

金：記得帶傘，下雨了。

唐納：真討厭。

❷ Ray: I forgot my homework.

Jake: **Not again**! It's the third time!

雷：我忘記帶作業了。

傑克：又來了！這是第三次了耶！

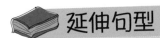 延伸句型　　 MP3 036

❶ learn about 學習

Learning about coffee making takes a lot of time.

學習製作咖啡需要花費許多時間。

❷ find out 找出（答案）

We will **find out** who commits the crime.

我們會把犯人揪出來。

❸ in array 列陣

Nine planets set **in array** in front of the Sun in the Solar system.　太陽系中，九個行星排列在太陽前方。

情境對話　 MP3 037

- Mr. Wang 王老師
- Ron 榮恩
- Kelly 凱莉

M: So do you have any pets? Ron, what do you say?

R: I have a cat. She is pure white, like snow.

M: I bet she is beautiful. What about you, Kelly?

K: I have a parrot. He is so talkative.

M: Did you guys teach him how to talk?

K: No. He just sort of learned words by listening to us talking.

王：你們有養寵物嗎？榮恩，你說說看。

榮：我有一隻貓，牠全身雪白。

王：它肯定很漂亮。凱莉，那妳呢？

凱：我有一隻鸚鵡，牠很聒噪。

王：妳有教牠說話嗎？

凱：沒有，牠似乎是聽我們講話，聽著聽著就會講了。

1 贏在起跑點——課堂知多少。

2 伴著孩子成長——親子教育。

Cat

延伸學習字彙

· quiet	安靜的
· fierce	凶狠的
· scary	嚇人的
· fluffy	毛茸茸的
· cuddly	討人喜歡的
· bouncy	活蹦亂跳的

Golden retriever

認識動物

· golden retriever	黃金獵犬
· Persian	波斯貓
· macaw	金剛鸚鵡
· goldfish	金魚
· rabbit	兔子
· hamster	倉鼠

what about you　那麼你呢

❶ I'm going to have Subway for lunch. **What about you**?

我要去 Subway 買午餐，你呢？

❷ Jenny is not coming for Christmas. **What about you**?

珍妮不會來過聖誕節，那你呢？

you guys 你們

❶ **You guys**! Hurry up!

你們幾個！動作快點！

❷ How are **you guys** doing?

你們好嗎？

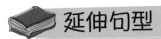 延伸句型  MP3 039

❶ what do you say 你說呢

Laura is thinking of opening a bakery. **What do you say**?

蘿拉考慮開一家烘焙坊。你覺得怎麼樣？

❷ I bet 我敢說

I bet Laura's store is gonna be a big hit.

我敢說蘿拉的店絕對會大受歡迎。

❸ sort of 似乎

Laura **sort of** has a lot of creative ideas of having a business.

蘿拉似乎對開店做生意很有想法。

Unit 14

Insect
昆蟲

· Mr. Wang 王老師
· Emma 艾瑪
· Laura 蘿拉

M: There are all kinds of insects around us. Who can give me an example?

王：我們身邊有很多種昆蟲。誰能舉例給我聽？

E: One time I saw a mantis on my father's car.

艾：有一次我在爸爸的車上看到螳螂。

M: That's kind of unusual. What did you do about it?

王：真少見。那妳拿牠怎麼辦呢？

E: I put it back in the grass.

艾：我把牠放回草叢裡。

M: How sweet. Anybody else?

王：妳真善良。還有人要舉例嗎？

L: I used to feed silkworms.

蘿：我以前有餵養蠶寶寶。

M: Right, they make babies like crazy.

王：對，牠們很會下蛋。

1 贏在起跑點——課堂知多少。

2 伴著孩子成長——親子教育。

Insect

延伸學習字彙

- flying　　　會飛的
- poisonous　有毒的
- larval　　　幼蟲的
- pupal　　　成蛹的
- custered　　群聚的
- stinging　　有針的

Gragonfly

認識昆蟲

- dragonfly　　蜻蜓
- moth　　　　蛾
- mantis　　　螳螂
- grasshopper　蚱蜢
- stag beetle　鍬形蟲
- flea　　　　跳蚤

 慣用語  MP3 041

all kinds of 各式各樣的

❶ In my wardrobe, I have **all kinds of** dress.
我的衣櫥裡有各種款式的洋裝。

❷ Peggy like **all kinds of** fruit.
佩姬喜歡各種水果。

....

give someone an example / an example of… 舉例/（某事）的例子

❶ **Give me an example of** the insects you learn today.
今天學了什麼昆蟲，舉個例子來聽聽。

❷ Mantis is **an example of** common insects.
螳螂是一種常見昆蟲。

 延伸句型　 MP3 042

❶ one time 有一次

One time Ronald fell down in front of everyone. Since then, he walks carefully.

有一次羅納在眾目睽睽之下跌倒，自此之後他走路總是很小心。

❷ do about… 處置；作出反應

What do I **do about** my dead silkworm?

我該怎麼處理死掉的蠶寶寶？

❸ how sweet 真善良；真貼心

How sweet is Emma to put the mantis back in the grass.

艾瑪把螳螂放回草叢裡，真是善良！

Mammal
哺乳動物

 情境對話　 MP3 043

- Mr. Peralta 普羅塔老師
- Emma 艾瑪
- Terry 泰瑞

E: I know that mammals are animals that don't lay eggs.

艾：我知道，哺乳動物就是不下蛋的動物。

M: That's not exactly correct, Emma. For instance, a platypus lays eggs.

普：艾瑪，妳這樣説不完全正確。像鴨嘴獸就會下蛋。

E: That doesn't count! A platypus is not a mammal!

艾：那不算！鴨嘴獸不是哺乳動物！

M: Face it Emma. Truth is not only platypuses are mammals, pangolins are mammals, too.

普：艾瑪，面對事實吧，不只鴨嘴獸，連穿山甲都是哺乳動物呢。

T: No way!

泰：不可能！

M: Alright kids, today I am going to blow your minds by introducing incredible mammals!

普：孩子們，今天我們要來認識不可思議的哺乳動物，準備大開眼界吧！

Mammal

延伸學習字彙

· clever	聰明的
· egg-laying	下蛋的
· viviparous	胎生的
· breast-feeding	哺乳的
· warm-blooded	恆溫的
· vertebrate	有脊椎的

Camel

認識哺乳動物

· platypus	鴨嘴獸
· gopher	地鼠
· pangolin	穿山甲
· camel	駱駝
· wild yak	氂牛
· antelope	羚羊

it counts / does not count　算數/不算數

❶ This is the third time I win over you and **it counts**!

這是我第三次贏過你了，別想耍賴。

❷ You **can't** possibly **count** that a win!

這樣也算贏？

....

face it　面對（現實）吧

❶ Let's **face it**, you don't know about mammals as much as you thought.

面對現實吧，你其實沒那麼了解哺乳動物。

❷ **Face it** Lucy, I can draw better than you.

露西，面對事實吧，我畫得比妳好。

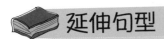 延伸句型　 MP3 045

❶ for instance 例如

Mammals can be very different in size, **for instance**, bats are the smallest and whales are the biggest.

哺乳動物的體型差異很大，例如蝙蝠是最小的，鯨魚是最大的。

❷ truth is 事實是

Truth is no matter what size they are in, mammals nurse their young with milk.

不過，事實上無論體型如何，哺乳動物都會以牛奶哺育牠們的孩子。

❸ not only…but (also) 不僅僅是…而且

Not only dogs or cats feed their babies, **but also** kangaroos, horses, lions, etc.

不只貓狗會哺育下一代，袋鼠、馬兒、獅子都是如此。

Unit 16 Photosynthesis
光合作用

 情境對話　 MP3 046

- Mr. Boyle 柏伊爾老師
- Gina 吉娜
- Terry 泰瑞

M: Kids, since we are going to National Botanic Garden this weekend, why don't we learn more about what plants do to live?

G: They depend on water solely.

M: No, Gina. Plants are huge contributors of fresh oxygen on planet Earth!

G: Do you mean they breathe out oxygen instead of carbon dioxide?

M: Maybe that sounds nonsense but it's absolutely right. It's called photosynthesis.

T: Little Terry didn't expect our excursion to be so scholarly.

柏：孩子們，既然我們這個週末要去國家植物園，何不來學習植物是如何生長的呢？

吉：植物有水就夠了。

柏：不，吉娜，植物是地球上最大的新鮮氧氣供應者。

吉：你是説植物吐氣時不是排出二氧化碳，而是氧氣嗎？

柏：聽起來可能很沒道理，但就是如此。這就是光合作用。

泰：小泰瑞沒想到校外教學這麼學術。

1 贏在起跑點—— 課堂知多少。

2 伴著孩子成長—— 親子教育。

延伸學習字彙

· botanical	植物學的
· botanic	植物界的
· biological	生物的
· organic	有機的
· inorganic	無機的
· circulating	循環的

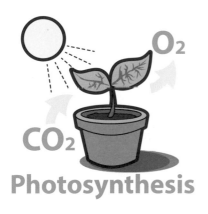

認識植物生理作用

· photosynthesis	光合作用
· cellular respiration	呼吸作用
· cell wall	細胞壁
· vascular bundle	維管束
· germination	萌芽
· phototropism	向光性

慣用語

why don't we… 我們何不…（用於提議）

❶ **Why don't we** have fried chicken for dinner?
我們何不吃炸雞當晚餐？

❷ It's raining. **Why don't we** stay home?
在下雨耶。我們何不待在家裡？

it's called 就是

❶ Plants have a system to carry nutrients and water. **It's called** vascular bundle.
植物有個輸送養分和水的系統。那就是維管束。

❷ Plants have a special protection to their cells. **It's called** cell wall.
植物的細胞有一層特殊的防護，也就是細胞壁。

延伸句型  MP3 048

❶ depend on 依靠

Plants **depend on** soil, water, and sun to grow.

植物仰賴土壤、水和陽光生長。

❷ breathe in / out 吸入/呼出

Human beings **breathe in** oxygen and **breathe out** carbon dioxide.

人類吸入氧氣，呼出二氧化碳。

❸ instead of 而不是

Plants breathe in carbon dioxide **instead of** oxygen.

植物吸入二氧化碳而非氧氣。

Electricity
電

 情境對話　 MP3 049

- Mr. Boyle 柏伊爾老師
- Gina 吉娜
- Terry 泰瑞

M: Kids, what's your least favorite thing when a typhoon strikes?

G: To have the electricity cut off.

M: Right! No one wants to be unable to have their smartphone charged. See how essential electricity is to our lives?

G: Why don't we just build a bunch of nuclear power plants in the country? Then we'll never have to worry about electricity going short.

M: Well, that's not possible. We have to consider renewable energy first.

柏：孩子們，颱風來襲時，你們最討厭發生什麼事？

吉：停電。

柏：沒錯，大家都希望可以幫智慧型手機充電。你們發現電對我們的生活有多重要了嗎？

吉：為什麼不在國內蓋一堆核電廠？這樣就永遠不用擔心電力不足了。

柏：這是不可能的，我們得先考慮使用再生能源才行。

T: I hope all that wind power generators work. It's making quite some noise out there.

泰：希望那些風力發電機有用。它們的噪音真的滿大的。

1 贏在起跑點──課堂知多少。

2 伴著孩子成長──親子教育。

Electricity

延伸學習字彙

- nuclear　　　　核能的
- thermal　　　　發熱的
- electric　　　　電流的
- renewable　　　可再生的

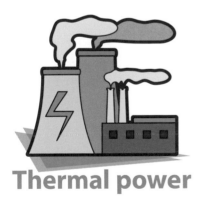

Thermal power

認識能源

- thermal power　　火力發電
- hydroelectric power
  水力發電
- wind power　　　風力發電
- solar energy　　　太陽能
- nuclear energy　　核能
- power plant　　　發電廠

least··· 最不

❶ Gina's **least** favorite thing is to have her smartphone taken away.

吉娜最討厭智慧型手機被拿走。

❷ Terry's **least** favorite activity is socializing.

泰瑞最討厭社交活動。

··

cut off 切斷；斷絕

❶ This village is totally **cut off** electricity for four days due to the typhoon.

這個村莊因為颱風整整斷電了四天。

❷ The army is **cut off** backups. They are going to lose the battle.

這個軍隊後援被切斷了，他們肯定要吃敗仗。

 延伸句型　 MP3 051

❶ be able to / unable to 可以/不可以做某事

Modern people **are able to** get a lot of services in 7-11.
現代人們能從 7-11 便利商店享受許多服務。

....

❷ have + p.p. 使…做某事

They can **have** packages **mailed**, bills **paid** and even clothes **washed** in 7-11.
他們可以在 7-11 寄包裹、繳帳單，甚至送洗衣物。

....

❸ go short 短缺

Entertainment rarely **goes short** for people nowadays.
如今人們不缺娛樂活動。

1 贏在起跑點——課堂知多少。

2 伴著孩子成長——親子教育。

Unit 18 Thermal expansion
熱漲冷縮

 情境對話   MP3 052

- Mr. Peralta 普羅塔老師
- Raymond 雷蒙
- Gina 吉娜

M: Class, how do you usually handle a jar that is hard to open? Like, it was screwed too tight.

普：同學，通常你們有罐子打不開怎麼辦？可能是蓋子轉太緊之類的。

R Break it with a hammer?

雷：用鐵鎚打破嗎？

M: No Ray! That's extremely dangerous! Can't you come up with some safer ideas?

普：雷，不可以！這樣太危險了！你就不能想一些安全一點的點子嗎？

R: Sometimes my mom uses a rag, and it works magically!

雷：有時候我媽會用抹布，就能神奇地打開了。

M: That's doable, too. Next time you can try soaking the cap part in hot water. It will pop open in no time.

普：這樣也可以。下次你可以試著將瓶蓋浸在熱水裡，就會馬上打開了。

G: I know thermal expansion.

吉：我知道熱漲冷縮。

When an object gets hot it expands, thus the cap opens up automatically.

物體受熱時體積會膨脹，所以蓋子才會自己打開。

1 贏在起跑點—— 課堂知多少。

2 伴著孩子成長—— 親子教育。

延伸學習字彙

· physical	物理的
· logical	邏輯的
· swollen	膨脹的
· shrinking	縮小的
· dynamic	動態的
· static	靜態的

認識物理現象

· thermal expansion	熱漲冷縮
· condensation	凝結
· melting	熔解
· evaporation	蒸發
· boiling	沸騰
· mirage	海市蜃樓

pop open / pop up （pop 是用來形容快速）立刻打開、立刻出現等等

❶ When you soak a jar in hot water, it will **pop up** in no time.

只要將罐子浸入熱水中，罐子就會立刻打開。

❷ Terry suddenly **popped up** in the party.

泰瑞突然現身派對。

··

open up 開啟；（引申義）坦白

❶ NYPD, **open up**!

我們是紐約警察，快開門！

❷ Gina **opened up** to Terry last night. She was sorry for being too proud.

吉娜昨晚對泰瑞坦白了，她對自己態度太驕傲感到抱歉。

延伸句型　MP3 054

❶ come up with 想出

Gina always **comes up with** creative ideas.
吉娜總是能想出創意十足的點子。

❷ in no time 立刻

When she has an idea, she'll practice it **in no time**.
她只要一有點子，就會立刻付諸實行。

❸ thus 因此

Gina is such an active person, **thus**, everyone likes to be around her.
吉娜總是這麼有活力，因此大家總喜歡圍繞在她身邊。

情境對話 MP3 055

· Mr. Peralta 普羅塔老師
· Michael 麥可
· Norman 諾曼

M: Who likes to go to the beach? Everybody, right?

普：誰喜歡到海邊去玩？大家都喜歡，對不對？

M: I love seeing tiny little crabs running around the muddy riverbed. They look pathetic and fragile.

麥：我喜歡小螃蟹在泥濘的河床上跑來跑去，看起來可憐又脆弱。

M: I hope you don't hurt those poor creatures. And no, that's a swamp, not beach.

普：希望你別傷害那些可憐的小動物，而且那是沼澤，不是海邊。

N: There were oyster farms on the beachside near my house.

諾：我家附近的海邊以前有養蚵。

M: That must be impressive, making a good use of that tidal range, right?

普：那肯定令你印象深刻，善用潮差作用，對不對？

N: All I could think of was the mouth-watering oyster omelet when I saw them.

諾：看到蚵仔的時候，我只想到好吃的蚵仔煎。

1 贏在起跑點——課堂知多少。

2 伴著孩子成長——親子教育。

Tide

延伸學習字彙

- tidal　　　　　　潮汐的
- muddy　　　　　　泥濘的
- repeated　　　　重複的
- regular　　　　　規律的
- astronomical　　天文的
- natural　　　　　自然的

Ebb

認識潮汐現象

- high water　　　滿潮
- low water　　　　乾潮
- flood　　　　　　漲潮
- ebb　　　　　　　退潮
- period of tide　潮汐週期
- tidal range　　　潮差

 慣用語  MP3 056

run around 跑來跑去

❶ The kitties are **running around** the table.
小貓在桌邊跑來跑去。

❷ Ants are **running around** the doughnut.
螞蟻在甜甜圈旁邊繞來繞區。

....

all I can think of / All I can do 我只想/我只能…

❶ **All I can think of** after a long day is to take a nap.
累了一整天之後，我只想好好睡一覺。

❷ The cake is in the oven. **All we can do** now is wait.
蛋糕已經進烤箱了。現在我們唯一能做的就是等待。

延伸句型 　MP3 057

❶ look + adj. 某人事物看起來

Little crabs running around on the mud **look fragile**.
在爛泥巴上跑來跑去的小螃蟹看起來很脆弱。

· ·

❷ it is impressive (that) 某人事物令人驚訝

It is impressive how strong life can be.
生命之強韌令人驚訝。

· ·

❸ make good use of 好好利用

Norman can really **make good use of** the freshly harvested oysters.
諾曼會善加烹調這些剛收成的蚵仔。

Embroidery
刺繡

 情境對話 MP3 058

· Ms. Santiago 聖蒂亞可老師
· Terry 泰瑞
· Gina 吉娜

M: Class, today we have to tap into our woman brain and learn how to put these amazing patterns on the cloth.

T: Little Terry doesn't possess a woman brain!

M: Yes, you do. Listen, embroidery is all about patience. Follow my instructions carefully, and don't hurt yourself with the sharp needles.

G: I think I'm not talented. It's a mess!

M: You'll be okay, Gina. Practice makes perfect.

G: Well, I guess I'll give it a try.

聖：同學，今天我們得發揮母性潛能，學習將這些美麗的圖案繡到布料上面。

泰：小泰瑞才沒有母性潛能呢！

聖：當然有，聽好，刺繡最講求耐心。小心遵從我的指示，別被尖銳的針刺傷了。

吉：我覺得我沒有天分，根本繡不好！

聖：吉娜，沒問題的，熟能生巧嘛。

吉：好吧，我再試試看。

Embroidery

延伸學習字彙

- complicated 　複雜的
- delicate 　　細緻的
- detailed 　　精細的
- traditional 　傳統的
- subtle 　　　巧妙的
- alive 　　　栩栩如生的

Textile

認識刺繡

- embroidery 　刺繡
- sewing 　　　縫紉
- patchwork 　拼布
- textile 　　　紡織品
- sewing needle 針頭
- string 　　　線

 慣用語  MP3 059

tap into… 運用；挑動

❶ Some people really know how to tap into others' emotions.

有些人很會動之以情。

❷ Businessmen know how to tap into consumers' pocket.

生意人對賺錢很在行。

....

all about… 最重要的是

❶ Learning embroidery is all about patience.

學刺繡最重要的是要有耐心。

❷ Study is all about perseverance.

念書最重要的是要有毅力。

 延伸句型　　　MP3 060

❶ someone is talented / gifted　某人很有天分

Ms. Santiago **is** very **talented** at embroidery.
聖蒂亞可老師在刺繡方面很有天分。

❷ practice makes perfect　熟能生巧

Don't give up too quickly. **Practice makes perfect**.
別輕易放棄，熟能生巧嘛。

❸ give it a try　試試看

Give it a try! Maybe it will turn out great.
試試看吧！也許結果會很不賴呢。

Handicraft
手工藝

 情境對話　 MP3 061

- Mr. Boyle 柏伊爾老師
- Gina 吉娜
- Terry 泰瑞
- Emma 艾瑪

M: Hi class, I have prepared all kinds of handicrafts for today's art class. You can choose your own craft to do.

柏： 同學，我為今天的美術課準備了很多不同的手工藝，大家可以自己選擇喜歡的。

G: I'd like to create a masterpiece out of papercutting!

吉： 我要用剪紙打造曠世傑作！

M: Very ambitious, Gina.

柏： 吉娜，妳很有雄心壯志唷。

T: I like pressed flower craft. This way I can keep the beauty of it forever.

泰： 我要玩押花，這樣就能把花朵的美麗永遠保存下來了。

Mr: Terry, I didn't know you are this sentimental.

柏： 泰瑞，我都不知道你這麼感性。

E: And I am about to create the most astounding Chinese knot of all time!

艾： 而我則是要做出前所未見的超美中國結！

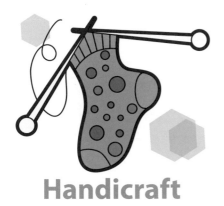

Handicraft

延伸學習字彙

- rustic　　　　質樸的
- unique　　　　獨特的
- dexterous　　靈巧的
- meaningful　　有意義的
- hand-made　　手工的
- old-school　　老式的

Chinese knotting

認識手工藝

- dyeing　　　　印染
- papercutting　剪紙
- carving　　　雕刻
- beading　　　串珠
- pressed flower craft　押花
- Chinese knotting　　中國結

one's own　某人自己的

❶ Gina wants to create a papercutting of **her own**.
吉娜想打造自己專屬的剪紙。

❷ Terry didn't have a pressed flour of **his own**, until he had this art class.
泰瑞沒有屬於自己的押花，直到他上了這堂美術課。

this way　這樣（就可以）

❶ We need to do handicraft more often. **This way** we will develop some sense of aesthetics.
我們應該常常做手工藝。這樣才能培養美學意識。

❷ You should go in the woods when you have time. **This way** the trees will help purify your body.
你有時間的話，應該常到森林裡走走。樹林會幫助你淨化身體。

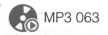 延伸句型　　MP3 063

❶ out of 出自

Out of Chinese culture born some everlasting crafts.
中國文化孕育了許多不朽的工藝。

❷ be about to 即將

Emma **is about to** create a beautiful Chinese knot.
艾瑪即將做出一個美麗的中國結。

❸ of all time 有史以來

Maybe it is the most beautiful Chinese knot **of all time**.
也許這就是有史以來最美的中國結。

Maya civilization
馬雅文明

 情境對話 MP3 064

- Mr. Wang 王老師
- Emma 艾瑪
- Terry 泰瑞

M: Class, do you know there are ancient civilizations around the world?

E: What does that mean?

M: Well, it means that these civilizations existed long, long time ago. Many have impacts on our civilization today, some just disappear for good.

T: Sounds creepy.

M: Once upon a time, there was a great empire called Maya, located in Central America. They worship a specific god "Kukulkan".

王：同學，你們知道世界上有很多古文明嗎？

艾：古文明是什麼？

王：古文明就是很久很久以前存在過的文明。許多影響了現代文明，有些則永遠消失。

泰：聽起來好令人毛骨悚然。

王：很久很久以前，有個強大的帝國叫馬雅，位在中美洲。馬雅人崇拜一種名叫「羽蛇神」的神明。

T: The name sounds scary.　　　　　泰：好可怕的名字。

1
贏在起跑點——
課堂知多少。

2
伴著孩子成長——
親子教育。

Civilization

延伸學習字彙

- ancient 　　　古老的
- mysterious 　神秘的
- historical 　　歷史的
- civilized 　　開化的
- uncivilized 　未開化的

Maya civilization

認識古文明

- Maya civilization 馬雅文明
- Inca Empire 　　印加帝國
- Aztec Empire 　阿茲特克帝國
- Babylon 　　　巴比倫
- Ancient Egypt civilization
  古埃及文明
- Aegean civilization
  愛琴文明

long time ago 很久以前

❶ Maya civilization was at its peak **long time ago**.

馬雅文明在很久以前達到頂峰。

❷ The whole civilization was destroyed **long time ago** by an unknown force.

整個文明在很久以前就被未知的力量摧毀了。

have impacts on 對⋯有影響

❶ Ancient civilizations usually **have impacts on** modern society.

古文明通常會對現代社會產生影響。

❷ Our behavior will **have impacts on** other classmates.

我們的行為會影響其他同學。

延伸句型  MP3 066

❶ for good 永遠

Some civilizations have disappeared **for good**.
有些文明已經永遠消失了。

. . . .

❷ sounds 聽起來

Traveling to Central America **sounds** quite challenging.
到中美洲旅行聽起來相當具挑戰性。

. . . .

❸ once upon a time 從前從前

Once upon a time, there was a girl named Cindcrella.
從前從前，有個女孩名叫仙杜瑞拉。

Israelites
以色列人

 情境對話　　 MP3 067　• Ms. Lin 林老師
• Emma 艾瑪

M: In the Middle East, there is a small yet powerful country called Israel. Do you know that this country is rebuilt not until 1948?

E: Did anything catastrophic happen to them before?

M: Yes, very devastating. The Israelites are one of the oldest ethnics recorded in Old Testament, way before other civilizations that we know today are established.

E: I heard that they still keep laws and regulations from old times.

M: Right, devout Jews still go in synagogues and study Torah

林：中東有個小而強盛的國家名叫以色列，你們知道這個國家是 1948 年才復國的嗎？

艾：在那之前，他們發生什麼慘事了嗎？

林：是的，相當慘烈。以色列人是舊約中所記載最古老的民族之一，遠比其他我們認識的文明還要早得多。

艾：我聽說他們仍遵行古時的律法和規條。

林：沒錯，虔誠的猶太人仍會上會堂，並仔細

carefully.

E: Sounds like they are like living in a different world.

研讀摩西五經。

艾：聽起來好像活在一個不同的世界。

Jerusalem

延伸學習字彙

· powerful	強盛的
· prosperous	繁榮的
· ethnic	民族的
· devout	虔誠的
· religious	宗教的
· strict	嚴格的

Judaism

認識以色列

· Judaism	猶太教
· Torah	摩西五經
· synagogue	會堂
· Golden lampstand	金燈台
· rabbi	
拉比（猶太教的智者）	
· Sabbath	安息日

Way / long + adj.　遠遠超過/早在（許久/長...）

❶ Way before Christ Jesus, the Israelites already have a deep relationship with Jehovah God.

早在耶穌基督以前，以色列人就與耶和華神有相當深的關係。

❷ Long after they are scattered, the Israelites finally rebuilt their country.

在以色列人四散到各地之後許久，以色列國終於重建了。

Live in different worlds 不同世界的人；差異很大

❶ No doubts, Jews and Muslins **live in different worlds**.

不諱言，猶太人和穆斯林的世界天差地遠。

❷ Westerners and Asians are like **living in different worlds**.

西方人和亞洲人差異相當大。

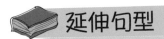 延伸句型　 MP3 069

❶ yet⋯ 但是；然而

Terry wants to play crane machine, **yet** he only has a bill.

泰瑞想玩夾娃娃機，但他只有一張鈔票。

❷ not until 直到

Not until he changes his bill into coins can he finally play it.

等他把鈔票換成硬幣，他才終於能玩了。

❸ from old times 古時候

Terry's parents still keep their concepts **from old times**, so they think Terry is wasting his money.

泰瑞的父母還保留著以前的觀念，所以他們認為泰瑞在浪費錢。

Crops: Rice
農作物：稻米

 情境對話   MP3 070 · Ms. Santiago 聖蒂亞可老師
· Jill 吉兒
· Ryan 雷恩

M: So rice has been one of the most consumed staple foods in the world. Especially for Asian people, rice is obviously indispensable in their daily life.

J: I love sushi. I can eat sushi every day.

M: That's very nice. It is said that sushi is very good for you; it's got zero oil and lots of fish.

R: I don't think having raw food every day is a good idea.

M: Good point Ryan. We also need vegetables, fruit and all kinds of different nutrients.

聖：稻米是世界上食用量最大的主食之一。特別對亞洲人而言，稻米顯然是每天不可或缺的食物。

吉：我愛壽司。我可以每天都吃壽司。

聖：非常好。據說壽司對身體有益，既不含油脂，又有大量魚類。

雷：我覺得每天吃生食不太好。

聖：雷恩，你說的沒錯。我們也需要攝取蔬菜、水果和各種不同的營養素。

J: Well, I don't mind having leftover sushi fried.

吉：我不介意把吃剩的壽司拿去炒。

Rice

延伸學習字彙

· daily	日用的
· staple	主要的
· critical	重要的
· necessary	必須的
· essential	不可或缺的
· dietary	飲食的

Sticky rice

認識稻米

· brown rice	糙米
· basmati rice	印度香米
· jasmine rice	泰國長米
· sticky rice	糯米
· wild rice	野生米
· sushi rice	壽司米

 **慣用語**  MP3 071

it's got… 含有

❶ Fish is good for health because **it's got** omega-3.

魚類對健康有益，因為魚肉含有 omega-3 不飽和脂肪酸。

❷ It is important to have a balance diet. **It's got** a huge influence to our life.

吃得均衡很重要。這對我們的生活影響重大。

....

good point 說得對；有道裡

❶ It is said that fish is good for our health, and I think it's a **good point**.

聽説魚肉對健康有益，我覺得很有道理。

❷ Jake: Hey! Quit eating steak and have fish instead!
Amy: **Good point**.

傑克：喂！別吃牛排了，改吃魚吧。
艾咪：你説得有道理。

 延伸句型　MP3 072

❶ one of 之一

Rice is **one of** the main crops in the world.
稻米是世界上主要的作物之一。

....

❷ it is said that 據說

It's said that there are more than one thousand types of rice.
據說稻米的品種超過一千種以上。

....

❸ don't mind doing 不介意做某事

Amy **doesn't mind** waking up in the morning to make her own breakfast.
艾咪不介意早起親手做早餐

1 贏在起跑點── 課堂知多少。

2 伴著孩子成長── 親子教育。

Crops: Wheat
農作物：小麥

 情境對話　 MP3 073

・Ms. Santiago 聖蒂亞可老師
・Jill 吉兒
・Ryan 雷恩

M: Last week, we took a peek into one of the most popular crops in the world: rice. Today we are going to know another crop that takes up the other half of the world!

聖：上週，我們學到世界上最受歡迎的穀物：稻米，今天要來認識另一種席捲半個世界的穀物！

J: I am not sure but are you talking about wheat?

吉：我是不太確定…但妳在説小麥嗎？

M: You are such a genius Jill!

聖：吉兒，妳真是個天才！

R: She is always so dramatic.

雷：我們的老師總是這麼誇張。

M: Everything you can name on breakfast table: waffle, pancake, bagel, muffin, loaf, are wheat products!

聖：一切在早餐桌上出現的食物： 格子鬆餅、煎餅、貝果、馬芬、吐司等等都是小麥產品。

J: Whao, I didn't know that we are taken over so thoroughly.

吉：哇，我都不知道小麥食品這麼普及。

1 贏在起跑點—課堂知多少。

2 伴著孩子成長—親子教育。

Wheat

延伸學習字彙

- common   常見的
- healthy   健康的
- unhealthy   不健康的
- allergic   過敏的
- refined   精緻的

Pasta

認識小麥製品

- pasta   義大利麵
- noodle   麵條
- bread   麵包
- bagel   貝果
- dumpling   水餃
- steamed bun   饅頭

take up　攻佔；（引申義）某物越來越多

❶ Pasta is **taking up** our pantry!
我們食物櫃裡的義大利麵越來越多了！

❷ Winter clothes are **taking up** Amy's closet.
艾咪衣櫃裡的冬季服裝越來越多了。

take over　佔領

❶ The weed is **taking over** in the wheat field.
小麥田裡雜草叢生。

❷ The King can't help but letting his enemy **take over** the castle.
國王不得不讓敵人佔領城堡。

延伸句型　🔊 MP3 075

❶ (take a peek) into… 偷看；（延伸義）認識…

When you peek **into** your diet, you will find way more wheat products than you thought.
如果你仔細檢視自己的飲食習慣，會發現小麥製品遠比你認為的多。

....

❷ talk about 談論

Nowadays Western people are **talking about** cutting down on wheat products.
現在西方世界興起減少攝取小麥製品的風潮。

....

❸ name 舉例說明

Name a wheat product and see if I have had it.
隨便說個小麥製品，看我有沒有吃過。

1 贏在起跑點——課堂知多少。

2 伴著孩子成長——親子教育。

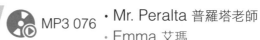

Unit 26

Greek mythology
希臘神話

 情境對話 🔊 MP3 076

- Mr. Peralta 普羅塔老師
- Emma 艾瑪
- Terry 泰瑞

M: Who has seen the latest movie Wonder Woman?

E: I did! I have made up my mind to be a wise, powerful, and charming woman like her!

M: Yep! Maybe when you grow up. That's a very inspiring character for sure.

T: I don't like her. Girls should not be too strong, or what are we boys supposed to do?

M: Clearly, you don't know that Wonder Woman is based on Diana, who is the goddess of hunting in Greek mythology.

普：誰看過強檔新片《神力女超人》？

艾：我看過！我也下定決心當個有智慧、強壯又有魅力的女性，就像她一樣！

普：很好！也許等妳長大以後。她的確是個激勵人心的角色。

泰：我不喜歡她。女生不應該太強壯，不然我們男生要幹嘛？

普：顯然你不知道神力女超人的故事是改編自黛安娜，也就是希臘神話中的狩獵女神。

E: Ha! There is no way to make the goddess of hunting hide behind men!

艾：哈！總不能叫狩獵女神躲在男生背後吧！

1 贏在起跑點——課堂知多少。

2 伴著孩子成長——親子教育。

Mythology

延伸學習字彙

· sly	狡猾的
· just	正義的
· wise	有智慧的
· greedy	貪婪的
· charming	有魅力的
· inspiring	激勵人心的

Zeus

認識希臘神話人物

· Zeus	眾神之王宙斯
· Diana	狩獵女神黛安娜
· Athena	戰爭女神雅典娜
· Hermes	冥界之神荷米斯
· Apollo	火神阿波羅
· Poseidon	水神波賽頓

 慣用語  MP3 077

for sure 當然；肯定是

❶ Athena is **for sure** the most known among all gods.
雅典娜肯定是眾神之中最有名的。

❷ The influence that Geek mythology has on Western culture is unmeasurable **for sure**.
希臘神話對西方文化的影響之大真是難以測量。

....

there is no way 不可能

❶ **There is no way** to understand Greek mythology in one day.
一天之內絕對不可能讀懂希臘神話。

❷ **There is no way** that a woman as powerful as Wonder Woman exists in the real world.
現實中絕不可能存在像神力女超人一樣強大的女性。

 延伸句型 🎧 MP3 078

❶ make up one's mind 下定決心

Emma has **made up her mind** to be like Wonder Woman when she grew up.
艾瑪決定在長大後成為像神力女超人一樣。

❷ be supposed to 應該

She **is supposed to** work out hard to have those muscles.
她得認真健身才能鍛鍊出一身肌肉。

❸ be based on 根據

Her motive **is** thoroughly **based on** her fantasy towards Wonder Woman.
她的動力完全來自對神力女超人的憧憬。

Part 2

伴著孩子成長－親子教育

生活是最好的老師，將英文融入生活中學得更快，把家打造成專屬你們的英語教室。在生活中一點一滴累積英文單字和句子，家中的每一個地方都是教材，天天開口說，建立自信心，親子一起快樂學習，一起共同成長！

Clean up the house
打掃家裡

D: Jack, while mom is preparing dinner, let's clean up the living room!

J: But dad, I'm still on my video games!

D: Come on son, give me a hand! I'll get the vacuum machine, and you can help me move chairs away.

J: Alright…only if you let me play for another 20 minutes after dinner.

D: I didn't teach you to be as tricky!

J: Well, last time you tricked me into taking out the garbage,

老：傑克，在媽媽煮晚餐的時候，我們來打掃客廳吧！

傑：爸爸，我還在打電動耶！

老：兒子，別這樣，幫幫忙吧。我去拿吸塵器，你幫我把椅子移開。

傑：好吧，但你得答應晚餐後再讓我玩二十分鐘。

老：我可沒教你變得這麼狡猾呀！

傑：上次你哄我幫你倒垃圾，但卻沒給我

and I didn't get the reward that you said you would give me.

答應好的獎勵耶。

Sweep the floor

延伸學習字彙

· clean	乾淨的
· tidy	整齊的
· messy	雜亂的
· filthy	骯髒的
· smelly	臭的
· organized	有秩序的

Mop the floor

一般家事

· sweep the floor	掃地
· mop the floor	拖地
· vacuum the carpet	吸塵
· do the laundry	洗衣服
· hang the clothes	晾衣服
· fold the clothes	摺衣服

慣用語

 MP3 080

come on 別這樣；少來

❶ **Come on**, let's clean up the kitchen together.
別這樣，跟我一起打掃廚房吧。

❷ **Come on**, don't be silly.
算了吧，別傻了。

give sb. a hand 幫助某人

❶ Jack, can you **give dad a hand**? He really needs your help.
傑克，你可以幫幫爸爸嗎？他真的很需要你的幫忙。

❷ I **gave my mom a hand** cooking dinner.
我幫忙媽媽煮晚餐。

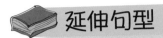  MP3 081

❶ clean up 打掃

Jack has to **clean up** his room today. It's a total mess!

傑克今天一定要打掃他的房間了。實在有夠亂！

❷ only if 除非

Jack will not clean up his room **only if** the girl he secretly likes is visiting.

除非他暗戀的女生到家裡來，否則傑克絕不會打掃房間。

❸ trick sb. into 哄騙某人做某事

Jack's father is planning on **tricking his son to** clean up his room.

傑克的爸爸打算哄騙他把房間打掃乾淨。

Unit 28 Table Setting 飯前準備

情境對話 MP3 082 ・Mom 媽媽 ・Jack 傑克

M: Dinner's ready! Jack, could you set the table for us?

J: Already done it mom!

M: Look at you! That's my good boy.

J: What's for dinner? Smells really nice!

M: I prepared your favorite chicken pot pie with potato salad.

J: Wow! Now I volunteer to do the dishes after meal!

媽：晚餐準備好了！傑克，你可以把餐具擺放整齊嗎？

傑：媽媽，我都弄好了。

媽：看看你！真是我的乖兒子。

傑：晚餐是什麼？聞起來好香喔。

媽：我煮了你最愛的雞肉深鍋派配馬鈴薯沙拉。

傑：哇！那我自願飯後洗碗！

1 贏在起跑點——課堂知多少。

2 伴著孩子成長——親子教育。

Tasty

延伸學習字彙

· tasty	美味的
· neat	整齊的
· bright	閃亮的
· fragrant	芬芳的
· shimmering	閃閃發光的
· mouthwatering	令人流口水的

Wipe the table

認識家事

· take out the trash	倒垃圾
· water the plants	澆花
· wipe the table	擦桌子
· set the table 在桌上放餐具	
· do the dishes	洗碗
· make the bed	鋪床

already + p.p. 早就做好某事/經歷過某事

❶ Dad wanted me to do the dishes, but I've **already done** it.

爸爸希望我洗碗，但我其實早就洗好了。

❷ Jack would like to have potato salad for dinner. Mom has **already made** it.

傑克晚餐想吃馬鈴薯沙拉，媽媽早就做好了。

....

volunteer to… 自願做某事

❶ Jack **volunteered to** do the dishes.

傑克自願洗碗。

❷ Dad **volunteered to** vacuum the carpet.

爸爸自願把地毯吸乾淨。

延伸句型  MP3 084

❶ could you / could you please…? （非常禮貌的）請問你可以…嗎？

Could you please set the table for us?
可以麻煩你佈置餐桌嗎？

❷ what's for breakfast / lunch / dinner / snack? 早餐/午餐/晚餐/點心是什麼？

What's for dinner? I'm starving!
晚餐是什麼？我餓壞了。

❸ smells good / bad / awful　聞起來好香/不好聞/好臭

Something **smells** really **good**! Are you baking?
有個味道好香喔！你在烘焙嗎？

Communication ❶
親子溝通❶

 情境對話 MP3 085

· Dad 老爸
· Jack 傑克

D: Jack, Mr. Smith said you fought with his son Carl again. What is going on?

J: He promised to lend me his skateboard, but didn't keep his promise.

D: Even so, you shouldn't punch him in his face.

J: He had it coming. He said I had no idea how to play a skateboard.

D: Jack, an eye for an eye is not a good way to solve problems. Now go apologize to Carl.

老: 傑克，史密斯先生說你又跟他兒子卡爾打架了。到底發生什麼事？

傑: 他答應要借我玩滑板，但是說話不算話。

老: 就算是這樣，你也不應該揍他的臉。

傑: 他活該。他說我根本不會玩滑板。

老: 傑克，以眼還眼不是好的解決方式。現在去跟卡爾道歉。

J: Okay. Maybe I did go too far.

傑：好吧。也許我做得太過火了。

延伸學習字彙

- guilty   內疚的
- irritated   易怒的
- impatient   沒有耐心的
- hot-tempered   性急的
- ashamed   羞愧的
- apologetic   歉意的

認識溝通方式

- talk   對談
- communicate   溝通
- negotiate   協商
- find balance   找到平衡
- make peace with   和好
- apologize   道歉

 慣用語  MP3 086

what is going on? 發生什麼事了？

❶ Carl had black eyes. **What is going on**?
卡爾有貓熊眼。怎麼會這樣？

❷ Why is everybody running out of the building?
What is going on?
為什麼大家都往外跑？發生什麼事了？

....

have it coming 自找的；活該

❶ Carl **had it coming**. He shouldn't tease Jack like that.
卡爾是自作自受，他不該那樣嘲笑傑克。

❷ Jack played in the rain and caught a cold. I guess he **had it coming**.
傑克在雨中玩耍，結果得了感冒。我想他是活該。

延伸句型　 MP3 087

❶ keep one's promise 遵守承諾

Dad always **keeps his promise** and gives me rewards.
老爸總會遵守諾言且給我獎勵。

❷ even so 儘管如此

Jack doesn't play skateboard well. **Even so**, he is very
fond of it.
傑克不太會玩滑板。儘管如此，他還是很愛玩。

❸ have no idea … 毫無頭緒

Jack **has no idea** that Carl is jealous of his skills.
傑克不知道卡爾偷偷忌妒他的技巧。

Communication ❷
親子溝通❷

M: Jack, that's the last meatball. Leave it to your sister.

J: How so? I'm bigger than her! I need more energy!

M: She is younger, and she can't compete with you. Since you're her brother, so you are responsible for taking care of her.

J: This is ridiculous.

M: Jack, before your sister was born, you are all alone. But now it's different. Do you see what I'm saying?

媽：傑克，那是最後一顆肉丸了。留給妹妹吃。

傑：為什麼？我塊頭比她大耶！我更需要營養！

媽：她年紀比你小，而且爭不贏你。既然你是哥哥，就有責任照顧妹妹。

傑：這不合理。

媽：傑克，在妹妹出生以前，只有你一個人，但現在情況不同了。你懂我的意思嗎？

J: Alright. There you go, sis.

傑：好啦，妹妹，給妳吃。

延伸學習字彙

Be aware of

· alone	孤獨的
· different	不同的
· ridiculous	荒唐的
· competitive	好勝的
· responsible	有責任感的
· irresponsible	沒有責任感的

認識照顧相關片語

Take care of

· take care of	照顧
· look after	看顧
· pay attention to	留意
· be aware of	注意
· be cautious to	謹慎
· stay focus	集中注意

  MP3 089

adj. + than 比較…

❶ Since Jack is **older than** his sister, he needs to take care of her.

因為傑克比妹妹年長，他必須照顧妹妹。

❷ Jack's father is **taller than** him.

傑克的爸爸比他高大。

---

do you see what I'm saying? 你明白我的意思嗎？

❶ Compete with your sister is childish. **Do you see what I'm saying**?

和妹妹爭是很幼稚的事。你懂我在說什麼嗎？

❷ Growing up means learning how to to give. **Do you see what I'm saying**?

長大意味著學習如何給予，你明白我的意思嗎？

延伸句型　 🔊 MP3 090

❶ compete with 競爭

Jack shouldn't **compete with** his own sister.
傑克不該與自己的妹妹爭。

....

❷ be responsible for 有責任

Instead, he **is responsible for** taking care of sister.
相反地，他有責任照顧妹妹。

....

❸ take care of 照顧

Jack **takes** good **care of** his sister when their parents are gone.
傑克在父母外出時用心照顧妹妹。

Unit 31 Draw with kids
陪孩子畫圖

 情境對話　 MP3 091　· Mom 媽媽
· Dolly 朵莉

D: Mommy, I'm so bored! I want to draw!

M: Alright honey. What do you have in mind? What do you want to draw?

D: A big house with shiny grass!

M: What about adding an apple tree with abundant apples?

D: I love apples so much!

M: Draw to your heart's content, honey. I know you're a talented angel.

朵：媽咪，我好無聊，我想畫畫。

媽：沒問題，甜心，妳有什麼想法？今天妳想畫什麼呢？

朵：一間大房子和閃耀的草地！

媽：要不要再加上結滿蘋果的蘋果樹呢？

朵：我好喜歡蘋果！

媽：寶貝，盡量畫。我知道妳是個有天分的天使。

Eraser

延伸學習字彙

- boring　　　　無趣的
- colorful　　　　繽紛的
- monotonous　　單調的
- imaginary　　　天馬行空的
- talented　　　　有天分的
- gifted　　　　　天賦異稟的

Crayon

認識繪圖用具

- paper　　　　　白紙
- eraser　　　　　橡皮擦
- pencil　　　　　鉛筆
- crayon　　　　　蠟筆
- color pen　　　　彩色筆
- color pencil　　　彩色鉛筆

 慣用語  MP3 092

have in mind 有…想法

❶ Where do you **have in mind**?
你在想甚麼？

❷ She told her mother what she **had in mind**.
她告訴她的母親她心裡想的是什麼。

....

talented 有天分的

❶ Dolly can draw really well since 3 years old. She is truly **talented**.
朵莉從三歲起就很會畫圖，她真的很有天分。

❷ Larry's son is so **talented**! He can hear a song and play it out!
賴瑞的兒子真有天分！他只要聽一遍歌曲，就能照彈一遍！

 延伸句型　　🔘 MP3 093

❶ sb. is bored. 某人感到無聊

Dolly is bored. She wants to draw so badly.
朵莉覺得無聊。她很想畫畫。

❷ sth. is boring. 某事物很無聊乏味

Jack thinks **drawing is boring**.
傑克覺得畫圖很乏味。

❸ to one's heart's content 盡情地

Dolly always draws **to her heart's content**.
朵莉總是要畫圖畫到盡興為止。

Unit 32

Read graphic books with kids
陪孩子讀繪本

 情境對話　 MP3 094
- Mom 媽媽
- Dolly 朵莉

M: Dolly, let's read this graphic book together. Look! The bears are all going to school!

D: Why do they have to go to school, mommy?

M: We all need to go to school. We need to learn knowledge from there, so we won't be ignorant. Besides, you will make lots of friends!

D: Will the teacher be kind to me?

M: If you are well- behaved, of course. Even if you are naughty, the teacher will teach you how to tell right from wrong.

媽：朵莉，我們一起讀這本繪本吧。看！小熊們都去上學了！

朵：媽咪，為什麼他們要去上學？

媽：我們都需要上學。去學校能學知識，這樣才不會什麼都不懂。而且，在學校還能交到很多朋友！

朵：老師會很親切嗎？

媽：如果妳守規矩的話，當然囉。即使妳調皮搗蛋，老師也會教妳分辨是非的。

D: Well, I guess I will like going to school. Hopefully, there will be some snack time!

朵：我想我會喜歡上學，希望有點心時間。

延伸學習字彙

· graphic	圖畫的
· ignorant	無知的
· child-friendly	適合兒童的
· storytelling	講故事的
· allegorical	有寓意的
· knowledgeable	博學的

Graphic book

認識各種刊物

· graphic book	繪本
· comic book	漫畫
· novel	小說
· poem	詩集
· magazine	雜誌
· newspaper	報紙

Comic book

behave oneself 守規矩

❶ If you don't **behave yourself**, there will be no cookies for you.

要是你不守規矩，你就不能吃餅乾。

❷ Dolly is a good kid. She always **behaves herself**.

朵莉是個乖寶寶。她總是非常守規矩。

....

tell right from wrong 明辨是非

❶ A teacher will teach students how to **tell right from wrong**.

老師會教導學生明辨是非。

❷ An infant doesn't know how to **tell right from wrong**.

嬰兒還不知道如何分辨是非。

延伸句型　　MP3 096

❶ make friends 交朋友

Dolly **made** many **friends** at school.
朵莉在學校交了許多朋友。

....

❷ be kind to 對⋯親切

She **is kind to** people, so everybody likes her.
她對別人都很友善，所以大家都喜歡她。

....

❸ even if 就算

Even if she makes mistakes, people forgive her immediately.
就算她犯了錯，人們也會馬上原諒她。

情境對話　 MP3 097

- Dad 老爸
- Jack 傑克
- Mom 媽媽

D: So Jack, I think we should work those fats after Thanksgiving. Do you agree?

老：所以傑克，我想感恩節過後我們該做運動減脂了，你說是不是？

J: Your belly is pretty incredible.

傑：你的肚子的確很可觀。

D: Hey! Stop picking on me. Let's do sit-ups first, and follow by push-ups and frog-jumps.

老：嘿！別再批評我了！首先我們來做仰臥起坐，然後再做伏地挺身和青蛙跳。

J: This is wearing me out, dad.

傑：老爸，這些動作累死我了。

D: Keep moving! You're burning calories!

老：繼續！脂肪在燃燒了！

M: Boys, after you're done,

媽：男孩們，你們運動

remember to drink plenty of water!

完後，記得多喝水喔。

1
贏在起跑點——
課堂知多少。

2
伴著孩子成長——
親子教育。

Sit-up

延伸學習字彙

· mild	和緩的
· intense	激烈的
· difficult	困難的
· relaxing	令人放鬆的
· burning	燃燒著的
· exhausting	令人精疲力竭的

Push-up

認識室內運動

· sit-up	仰臥起坐
· push-up	伏地挺身
· squat	深蹲
· lunge	跨步蹲
· wall sit	無影凳
· plank	肘撐

work those fats 動動身體消脂

❶ Time to **work those fats** and get fit.

是時候運動健身了。

❷ You really should consider **working those fats**!

你真的該好好考慮運動減肥了！

....

follow by 接著是

❶ A cycle of the 7-minute workout starts from 7 sit-ups and **follows by** 7 push-ups.

七分鐘健身從七下仰臥起坐開始，接著是七下伏地挺身。

❷ A romantic date is usually **followed by** a great dinner.

一場浪漫的約會通常會以美妙的晚餐做結。

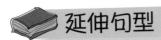 延伸句型　 MP3 099

❶ pick on sb. 找碴

Jack was **picking on his** father's body.
傑克對他爸爸的身材挑三揀四。

．．

❷ wear sb. out 使某人累慘

Intense exercise **wore Jack out**.
激烈運動讓傑克累慘了。

．．

❸ plenty of 大量的

Remember to drink **plenty of** water after exercise.
運動完記得補充大量水分。

Outdoor exercise
戶外運動

 情境對話　 MP3 100

- Dad 老爸
- Jack 傑克

D: Time for roller skating! Jack, did you bring your skates?

J: I did! And I am ready to roll.

D: Speaking of roller skating, do you know who won the golden medal at the 29th International University Sports Federation?

J: If my memory serves me right, it was a girl from Taiwan.

D: Yep. Thanks to her coach's advice at the last minute, she changed her skates to smaller rollers and won the race.

J: I want to be a skater like that, too!

老：該去練滑輪了！傑克，你帶好直排輪了嗎？

傑：帶了！我準備好好練習了。

老：說到滑輪，你知道誰奪下第 29 屆世大運滑輪金牌嗎？

傑：我沒記錯的話，是個台灣女生吧。

老：沒錯。多虧了教練在最後一分鐘要她換上小滑輪，她順利奪得冠軍。

傑：我也想當這樣的滑輪選手！

Skateboarding

延伸學習字彙

- individual   單人的
- group   團體的
- indoor   室內的
- outdoor   戶外的
- skillful   熟練的
- well-trained   鍛鍊有加的

Archery

認識戶外運動

- archery   射箭
- horseback riding   騎馬
- football   美式足球
- hockey   曲棍球
- roller skating   滑輪
- skateboarding   溜滑板

ready to roll 準備好大展身手（不一定與滑輪相關）

❶ I am fully prepared, and I'm **ready to roll**.
我已經做好萬全的準備，要來大展身手了。

❷ The path is clear. Are you **ready to roll**?
跑道淨空了，準備大展身手了嗎？

last minute 最後一刻

❶ Jack likes to change plans at the **last minute**.
傑克總喜歡在最後一刻變卦。

❷ It's the **last minute** ticket. Do you want to book it?
這是截止前最後的票了。你要訂嗎？

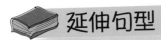 延伸句型  MP3 102

❶ speak of 說到

Speaking of roller skating, Taiwan is a competent country.
説到滑輪運動，台灣實力堅強。

❷ thanks to 幸虧

Thanks to the coach's advice, Taiwanese athlete was able to win the golden medal.
多虧教練的建議，台灣選手順利奪下金牌。

❸ if my memory serves me right 如果我沒記錯的話

If my memory serves me right, I have been practicing roller skating for five years!
如果我沒記錯的話，我已經練習滑輪五年了！

151

Appearance
描述外表

J: Dad, I found my classmate Amy really attractive. She has this long curly hair. It's smooth, shiny and breathtaking!

傑：老爸，我覺得我的同學艾咪好迷人喔。她有一頭長捲髮，又柔軟又閃耀，令我覺得屏息！

D: Is she blond?

老：她是不是金髮碧眼？

J: No, she has black hair, but it doesn't matter. I can't help but being drawn to her!

傑：不，她是黑髮，但我一點也不介意。她真是太吸引我了！

D: Seems like you're truly in love.

老：聽起來你真的戀愛了。

J: I don't even care that she's a bit chubby…I think she is the one.

傑：我甚至不在乎她有一點圓圓胖胖的…我想她就是我的真

命天女。

D: Well, maybe you should ask her out.

老：也許你應該約她出去。

Chubby

延伸學習字彙

- attractive   迷人的
- curly   捲曲的
- smooth   柔順的
- shiny   閃耀的
- breathtaking   令人驚嘆的
- chubby   胖胖的

Freckle

認識各種外表詞彙

- curly hair   捲髮的
- bald   禿頭的
- freckle   雀斑
- robust   健壯的
- slender   苗條的
- boney   骨感的

 慣用語  MP3 104

in love 戀愛了

❶ Jack is **in love** with Amy, his classmate.
傑克愛上他的同學艾咪了。

❷ He is not sure if Amy is **in love** with him, too.
他不確定艾咪是否也喜歡他。

she / he is the one 真命天子/天女

❶ Amy is so cute. Jack thinks that **she is the one** for him.
艾咪超可愛。傑克認為她就是他的真命天女。

❷ Although you all think Jack is too serious, I believe **he is the one** for me.
雖然你們都覺得傑克很嚴肅，但我相信他是我的真命天子。

延伸句型　　MP3 105

❶ can't help but 不得不

Jack **can't help but** falling in love with Amy.
傑克情不自禁愛上艾咪。

❷ seems like 似乎

It **seems like** there is nothing that can stand in his way.
似乎沒有任何事阻止得了他的感情。

❸ ask sb. out 約某人出去

Jack is determined to **ask Amy out**.
傑克決定約艾咪出門約會。

Unit 36

Emotion
描述情緒

 情境對話 MP3 106

· Mom 媽媽
· Jack 傑克

M: Jack, what's going on? Why are you not as energetic as usual?

J: Mom, I told Amy I liked her, but she said she didn't feel the same way.

M: Oh, I'm sorry, son.

J: Now I think it's the end of the world.

M: Nonsense. You've got so much ahead waiting for you.

J: I think you're right. I still have my potential. I will try my best to make Amy love me back!

媽： 傑克，怎麼了？你怎麼不像平常那麼有精神？

傑： 媽媽，我跟艾咪告白，但她說她對我沒有那種感覺。

媽： 兒子，我很遺憾。

傑： 現在我覺得一切都完了。

媽： 胡說，還有大好前程等著你呢。

傑： 我想妳說的沒錯，我還大有可為。我要努力讓艾咪喜歡上我！

Smile

延伸學習字彙

- agitated — 激動
- thrilled — 欣喜若狂
- furious — 狂怒
- confused — 困惑
- depressed — 沮喪
- disappointed — 失望

Tear

情緒反應

- sadness — 悲傷
- tear — 眼淚
- rage — 怒氣
- happiness — 幸福感
- smile — 微笑
- laughter — 笑聲

as usual 老樣子；像平常一樣

❶ **As usual**, Jack is late for school again.
老樣子，傑克上學又遲到了。

❷ However, today Amy is not as calm **as usual**.
不過，今天艾咪卻不如往常冷靜。

feel the same way 有一樣的感情（通常指愛情）

❶ Jack likes Amy, but she doesn't **feel the same way** for him.
傑克喜歡艾咪，但是郎有意妹無情。

❷ You are a good guy, but I don't **feel the same way** for you.
你是個好人，但我只把你當朋友。

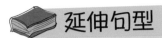  MP3 108

❶ end of sth. 末日；完蛋了

Breaking up isn't the **end of the world**.
分手不是世界末日。

❷ sth. is ahead waiting for you 大好前程

A good life is ahead waiting for me.
我還有大好前程在等著我呢。

❸ try my best 盡我所能

You should **try your best** to cheer yourself up.
你應該盡力讓自己快樂起來。

情境對話 MP3 109 ・Mom 媽媽
・Jack 傑克

M: You had better find some hobbies, so you can get over with Amy.

J: Well, I love gaming.

M: Other than that, do you want to try reading novels, too? Harry Potter is a good choice.

J: Magic world and all that? No thanks.

M: What about gardening? You've always loved helping grandpa in the field.

J: Sounds fun. Maybe I can grow some carrots and potatoes.

媽：你最好培養一些嗜好，好把艾咪忘掉。

傑：我喜歡打電動。

媽：除此之外，要不要試著讀小說呢？《哈利波特》是個不錯的選擇。

傑：魔法世界這一些嗎？不了，謝謝。

媽：那園藝呢？你一直都很喜歡下田幫忙爺爺。

傑：聽起來不錯，也許我可以種些紅蘿蔔和馬鈴薯。

1 贏在起跑點──課堂知多少。

2 伴著孩子成長──親子教育。

Gardening

延伸學習字彙

- exciting　　令人興奮的
- relaxing　　令人放鬆的
- soothing　　撫慰人心的
- addictive　　令人上癮的
- obsessed　　令人著迷的
- enchanting　令人醉心的

Exercising

各種嗜好

- reading　　閱讀
- baking　　烘焙
- cooking　　料理
- gardening　園藝
- gaming　　打電玩
- exercising　做運動

 慣用語  MP3 110

good choice 好選擇

❶ If you want to start reading, Harry Potter is a **good choice**.

如果你想開始閱讀的話，《哈利波特》是個好選擇。

❷ If you want to do exercise without sweating, walking is a **good choice**.

如果你想運動又不想流汗，走路是個不錯的選擇。

....

and all that (kind of stuff) 之類的

❶ Jack doesn't like magic **and all that**.

傑克不喜歡跟魔法有關的題材。

❷ Packing **and all that** is a nightmare, so I never go camping.

打包行李之類的很麻煩，所以我從不去露營。

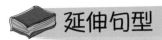 延伸句型　　 MP3 111

1
贏在起跑點──
課堂知多少。

2
伴著孩子成長──
親子教育。

❶ had better 最好

Jack **had better** find something else to do, or he will keep thinking about Amy.

傑克最好找點別的事情來做，否則他會對艾咪念念不忘。

....

❷ get over with 忘掉；釋懷

It's the best that he **gets over with** her ASAP.

他最好盡快把她忘了。(ASAP: as soon as possible)

....

❸ other than 除了⋯之外

Other than dating girls, Jack should focus on study more.

與其忙著談戀愛，傑克不如認真念書。

情境對話  MP3 112

- Mom 媽媽
- Jack 傑克
- Dad 爸爸

M: Aren't you boys supposed to be gone for roller skating by now?

J: It's raining cats and dogs outside, so dad and I decided to stay inside.

M: Oh, that's too bad.

J: I know. It sucks.

D: What don't we play board games? We can brainstorm together while it's storming outside.

M: That's a good one. Since it's wet and cold, I'll make you guys some chocolate chip cookies!

媽： 你們怎麼還在這裡？不是應該出門練習滑輪了嗎？

傑： 外面下著傾盆大雨，所以爸爸和我決定待在家裡。

媽： 喔，這真是太糟了。

傑： 我知道，糟透了。

爸： 我們何不玩桌遊呢？外面在下狂風暴雨，我們可以進行腦力激盪。

媽： 這個主意不錯。既然天氣又冷又濕，不如我來烤些巧克力豆餅乾吧！

Windy

延伸學習字彙

· stifling	悶熱的
· humid	潮濕悶熱的
· damp	濕冷的
· bracing	天氣舒適的
· chilly	有點涼意的
· freezing	冷澈心扉的

Cloudy

認識天氣

· sunny	晴天
· rainy	雨天
· windy	有風的日子
· cloudy	陰天
· snowy	下雪
· hurricane	颶風

1 贏在起跑點——
課堂知多少。

2 伴著孩子成長——
親子教育。

it sucks 糟透了

❶ It sucks that I can't go practice roller skating.

不能去練習滑輪真糟糕。

❷ I lost my pencil today. **It** really **sucks**.

今天我把鉛筆弄丟。真是糟透了。

....

that's a good one. 說得好；好主意

❶ Dad suggests that we stay home and bake cookies. **That's a** really **good one**!

老爸建議我們在家烤餅乾。真是個好主意。

❷ Jack: Although we didn't get to practice today, we were lucky to avoid the rain.

Dad: **That's a good one**!

傑：雖然我們今天沒辦法練習，但好在我們也躲過了大雨。

老爸：你說得沒錯！

 延伸句型　　🔊 MP3 114

❶ gone for 出門去⋯

It's 8 o'clock. Amy should have **gone for** school.
已經八點了。艾咪早該出門上學了。

⋯⋯⋯⋯⋯⋯⋯⋯⋯⋯⋯⋯⋯⋯⋯⋯⋯⋯⋯⋯⋯⋯⋯⋯⋯⋯⋯⋯

❷ by now 現在

If she left home on time, she should have got to school **by now**.
要是她準時出門，現在早該到學校了。

⋯⋯⋯⋯⋯⋯⋯⋯⋯⋯⋯⋯⋯⋯⋯⋯⋯⋯⋯⋯⋯⋯⋯⋯⋯⋯⋯⋯

❸ it's raining cats and dogs 傾盆大雨

However, **it was raining cats and dogs**, so Amy couldn't leave the house as planned.
可惜的是，外頭下著傾盆大雨，艾咪無法按照時間出門。

Unit 39

Transportation
交通工具

M: Jack, for your coming roller skating competition, we are taking the train.

J: Wow, it's my first time to be on a train. I can't wait!

M: Keep in mind that once we are on the train, there's no turning back. So make sure you bring everything with you.

J: Don't worry mom; I got it covered.

M: Hey, we can have railway bento if you want.

J: The legendary railway bento? Of course!

媽：傑克，對於你即將到來的滑輪比賽，我們會搭火車去。

傑：哇，這是我第一次搭火車耶。我等不及了！

媽：記住，一旦上了火車就不能中途回家，所以東西可都要帶好才行。

傑：媽媽，別擔心，交給我就對了。

媽：嘿，如果你想的話，我們可以買鐵路便當。

傑：傳說中的鐵路便當？當然想！

1 贏在起跑點 課堂知多少。

2 伴著孩子成長 親子教育。

Ferry

延伸學習字彙

- convenient　　　方便的
- urban　　　　　市區的
- suburban　　　　郊區的
- continuous　　　連貫的
- rapid　　　　　快速的
- touristic　　　　觀光的

Aerial lift

認識交通工具

- MRT (Mass Rapid Transit)
  大眾捷運系統
- metro　　　　　地鐵，捷運
- ferry　　　　　渡輪
- high speed rail　高速鐵路
- tram　　　　　路面電車
- aerial lift　　　纜車

 **慣用語**  MP3 116

coming 即將到來的

❶ Jack is having a competition in the **coming** weekend.

這個週末傑克要參加比賽。

❷ Mom is preparing food for the **coming** picnic.

媽媽為即將到來的野餐活動準備食物。

⋯⋯⋯⋯⋯⋯⋯⋯⋯⋯⋯⋯⋯⋯⋯⋯⋯⋯⋯⋯⋯⋯⋯⋯

can't wait 等不及了

❶ Jack **can't wait** to be on the train.

傑克等不及要坐火車了。

❷ It is said that railway bento is very delicious. Jack **can't wait** to try it.

據說鐵路便當非常好吃。傑克等不及要試試了。

 延伸句型 MP3 117

❶ the first time 第一次

It is his **first time** to be on a train.

這是他第一次坐火車。

....

❷ make sure 確認

Make sure to bring your train ticket before you get on the train.

上火車之前，記得帶上火車票。

....

❸ get it covered 交給我就對了

No need to worry. Dad has **got it covered**.

別擔心。一切交給爸爸就對了。

171

Family trip
家族旅行

 情境對話　 MP3 118
- Dad 老爸
- Jack 傑克

D: This coming weekend we should go for a family trip. Which one do you prefer, the ocean or the mountain?

老：這個周末我們應該來一次家族旅行。你比較想去海邊，還是去山上？

J: I surely want to go in the mountains! But if we can go fishing, that'd be interesting, too.

傑：我當然想去山上！不過，如果能去釣魚，那也很有趣。

D: Well, you've got to make a decision.

老：你得做出選擇。

J: Is there a way that I can do it both?

傑：我有可能兩個地方都去嗎？

D: You cannot sell the cow and drink the milk. Just pick one.

老：魚與熊掌不可兼得啊。就選一個吧。

J: I think the idea of camping prevails. That'd be my dream comes true.

傑：我想我還是比較想去露營。這會像是我的夢想成真。

1
贏在起跑點——
課堂知多少。

2
伴著孩子成長——
親子教育。

Camping

延伸學習字彙

- cozy　　　　　　舒適的
- fresh　　　　　　新鮮的
- family　　　　　　家族的
- heartwarming　　溫馨的
- harmonious　　　和樂的
- adventurous　　　探險的

Barbecue

認識家庭旅行活動

- mountain climbing　登山
- hiking　　　　　　健行
- fishing　　　　　　釣魚
- camping　　　　　露營
- bike-riding　　　　騎腳踏車
- barbecue　　　　　烤肉

you cannot sell the cow and drink the milk. 魚與熊掌不可兼得

❶ If you want to go fishing, then you can't go hiking in the mountain. **You cannot sell the cow and drink the milk**.

如果你想釣魚，那就不能去爬山。魚與熊掌不可兼得呀。

❷ Playing all day will not get you good grades. **You cannot sell the cow and drink the milk**.

整天玩樂是不可能有好成績的。魚與熊掌不可兼得。

a dream comes true. 夢想成真

❶ Going fishing with my dad is **a dream comes true for me**.

跟爸爸一起釣魚，對我來說是夢想成真。

❷ If I can travel to Japan, that'll be **a dream comes true**!

如果我能去日本旅行，那將會是美夢成真！

延伸句型  MP3 120

❶ you've got to… 你必須

You've got to choose one destination for the family trip.
你得為家族旅行選一個目的地。

❷ make a decision 做出決定

It's hard, but I have to **make a decision**.
雖然不容易，但我必須做出抉擇。

❸ sth. / sb. prevails 某事/人獲勝

At the end, the thought of going fishing **prevails**.
最後，我還是比較想去釣魚。

Unit 41

Greeting
打招呼

・Dad 老爸
・Jack 傑克

J: What's for breakfast?

D: Before that, didn't you forget to say something?

J: Errr…Is it a good sign that Dolly is not crying?

D: What about "good morning, daddy"?

J: Right! It's not like we haven't seen each other for years.

D: Doesn't matter if we see each other every day, or how familiar we are with each other; never forget your manner.

傑：早餐吃什麼？

老：在此之前，你是不是忘了說什麼話？

傑：呃…朵莉沒哭，這是個好預兆？

老：「老爸早安」如何？

傑：唉！又不是我們幾年沒見了。

老：不論我們是不是每天見面，也不管我們對彼此多熟悉，禮貌永遠不可少。

Greeting

Friendly

延伸學習字彙

- polite　　　　有禮貌的
- modest　　　 謙虛的
- friendly　　　友善的
- proud　　　　驕傲的
- impolite　　　沒有禮貌的
- well-behaved　行為得當的

日用招呼語

- good morning　早安
- good afternoon　午安
- good evening　晚上好
- good night　　晚安
- have a good one
  祝你有美好的一天
- see you　　　　再見

177

a good sign 好兆頭

❶ The sun came out! This is **a good sign**.
太陽出來了！這是個好兆頭。

❷ It is **a good sign** that the baby is not crying.
寶寶沒哭真是好預兆。

....

(something) doesn't matter 不在乎

❶ **Doesn't matter** if it's rainy or not, Jack has to practice roller skating.
不管有沒有下雨，傑克都必須練習滑輪。

❷ Dad's opinion **doesn't matter** that much. Mom is the boss in the house.
老爸的意見不重要，媽媽才是當家作主的人。

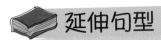 延伸句型　 MP3 123

❶ what about　認為⋯如何

What about having pancakes for breakfast?
吃鬆餅當早餐怎麼樣？

❷ it's not like　又不是

It's not like we don't have any choice, why pancake?
又不是我們沒別的選擇，何必吃鬆餅？

❸ familiar with 對⋯熟悉

I'm **familiar with** the recipe.
我對鬆餅的做法瞭如指掌。

Unit 42 **Family members**
家族成員

• Luke 路卡
• Jack 傑克
• Aunt Becky 貝琪阿姨

L: Jack! Long time no see!

J: Yeah, since last Christmas, I guess?

L: You must remember my little sister, Karen. She just turned two, my dad decided to put Elizabeth as her middle name.

J: In honor of grandma? That's fantastic.

A: Hi Jack, Merry Christmas.

J: Aunt Becky, you are still so radiant. You never get old!

路：傑克，好久不見。

傑：是啊，我想是從去年聖誕節過後吧？

路：你一定記得我的小妹凱倫。她才剛滿兩歲，我爸決定把她的中間名字取為伊莉莎白。

傑：是為了紀念祖母嗎？太棒了。

貝：嗨，傑克，聖誕快樂。

傑：貝琪阿姨，妳還是這麼容光煥發，都不會變老。

1
贏在起跑點——
課堂知多少。

2
伴著孩子成長——
親子教育。

延伸學習字彙

Parents

· close	親近的
· distant	遠房的
· elder	比較年長的
· little	比較年輕的
· respectful	尊敬的
· honorable	值得敬重的

認識家族成員

Grandparents

· parents	雙親
· grandparents	祖父母
· sibling	手足
· uncle	叔伯
· aunt	阿姨
· cousin	堂表兄弟姊妹

long time no see 好久不見

❶ **Long time no see**! Jack, you have grown taller.
好久不見！傑克，你長高了。

❷ **Long time no see**. It has been a year at least.
好久不見，至少一年了。

I guess so. 我想是吧

❶ Uncle said I've grown taller. **I guess so**.
叔叔說我長高了，我想是吧。

❷ People often say that drinking milk helps to grow up. **I guess so**.
人們常說喝牛奶有助長高，我想應該沒錯。

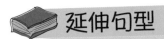 延伸句型  MP3 126

❶ you must remember 一定記得

You must remember my daughter Molly.
你一定記得我的女兒茉莉。

---

❷ just turned + number 剛滿⋯歲

She **just turned 17**.
她才剛滿 17 歲。

---

❸ in honor of⋯ 紀念⋯

Peter named his daughter Molly **in honor of** his sister.
彼得為女兒取名茉莉以紀念他的姊姊。

Visiting a museum
參觀博物館

 情境對話 MP3 127
· Mom 媽媽
· Jack 傑克

M: Jack, this is the famous sculpture "The Thinker". See that facial expression? Its face, muscle, and position are very well sculpted.

J: What makes it a great piece of art?

M: It is a symbol of human life. Sometimes we have anguishes, not to mention our daily worries.

J: I see. In other words, if I am lucky enough to play video games today, I may become an art named "The Happy

媽：傑克，這就是著名的雕像「沉思者」，看到它的表情了嗎？它的臉部、肌肉和動作都雕刻得很細緻。

傑：是什麼使得這個藝術作品會出名呢？

媽：因為它是人類生活的象徵。有時候我們會苦惱，更別提每天許多令人操心的事。

傑：我懂了。也就是說，如果我今天幸運能打電動的話，我也可能成為名叫

Man".

M: You stand a chance.

「快樂人」的藝術
作品。

媽：也是有可能啦。

1 贏在起跑點——
課堂知多少。

2 伴著孩子成長——
親子教育。

National Palace Museum

延伸學習字彙

· artistic	藝術的
· aesthetic	美學的
· abstract	抽象的
· classical	古典的
· visualized	視覺化的
· contemporary	當代的

認識知名博物館

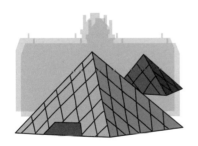

Louvre

· National Palace Museum
故宮博物院（台灣）

· British Museum
大英博物館（英國）

· Museum of Modern Art
現代藝術博物館（美國）

· Louvre
羅浮宮（法國）

 慣用語 MP3 128

in other words 換句話說

❶ It's rainy outside. **In other words**, it's better to stay home.

外面在下雨，也就是説，最好待在家裡。

❷ Jack likes to play video games. **In other words**, he is not a fan of study.

傑克喜歡打電動。換句話説，他不太愛念書。

....

stand a chance 有機會

❶ Jimmy doesn't **stand a chance** to snack on that apple pie.

吉米完全沒機會對那塊蘋果派下手。

❷ Lauran doesn't **stand a chance** to sneak out without being noticed.

羅倫沒辦法偷溜出門而不被發現。

 延伸句型　 MP3 129

❶ what makes it⋯ 是什麼使得⋯

What makes playing computer games so important?

是什麼讓玩電腦遊戲這麼重要？

⋯⋯⋯⋯⋯⋯⋯⋯⋯⋯⋯⋯⋯⋯⋯⋯⋯⋯⋯⋯⋯⋯⋯⋯⋯

❷ a symbol of 象徵

Doves are **symbols of** peace.

鴿子是和平的象徵。

⋯⋯⋯⋯⋯⋯⋯⋯⋯⋯⋯⋯⋯⋯⋯⋯⋯⋯⋯⋯⋯⋯⋯⋯⋯

❸ not to mention 更別提

It's impossible to go out in this kind of rain, **not to mention** practicing roller skating.

這麼大的雨是不可能出門的，更別提去練滑輪了。

情境對話　 MP3 130

- Dolly 朵莉
- Mom 媽媽
- Dad 老爸

D: Mommy, can I help out?

M: Sweetheart, you can prepare the eggs. Crack them and beat them together, just like this.

D: The yolks and the whites are all mixed up!

M: That's what it takes to make a good omelet. It's a piece of cake, isn't it?

D: Is my angel giving a hand or is she making a mess?

M: She will be the next head chef.

朵：媽咪，我可以幫忙嗎？

媽：甜心，妳可以準備雞蛋。先打蛋再攪拌，就像這樣。

朵：蛋黃和蛋白都混在一起了。

媽：這是製作美味煎蛋捲的必要步驟，很簡單，不是嗎？

爸：我的小天使是在幫忙，還是在幫倒忙？

媽：她會成為下一任天菜大廚唷。

1
贏在起跑點——
課堂知多少。

2
伴著孩子成長——
親子教育。

Stove

延伸學習字彙

· precise	精確的
· accurate	正確的
· cautious	小心的
· attentive	謹慎的
· heated	加熱的
· frozen	冷凍的

Steamer

常用廚房電器

· oven	烤箱
· stove	瓦斯爐
· steamcr	電鍋
· blender	果汁機
· microwave	微波爐
· dish-washer	洗碗機

a piece of cake 輕而易舉

❶ Making an omelet is **a piece of cake**.

製作煎蛋捲是一件輕而易舉的事。

❷ Finishing assignment before school is **a piece of cake**.

放學前把功課做完真是輕而易舉。

....

give someone a hand 出手幫忙

❶ Judy, I'm having some problems here. Can you **give me a hand**?

茱蒂，我遇到一些麻煩了，可以幫我一下嗎？

❷ Dolly **gave her mother a hand** and that makes her really happy.

朵莉幫上媽媽的忙，這讓媽媽非常開心。

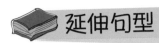 延伸句型　 MP3 132

❶ help out 幫忙

When it comes to cooking, Dolly likes to **help out**.
說到烹飪，朵莉很喜歡幫忙。

....

❷ mix up 混在一起

The green beans and red beans are **mixed up**. How can I distinguish these two?
綠豆和紅豆混在一起了，我該怎麼區分它們？

....

❸ what it takes to⋯ 必要的方法⋯

Good visual abiliy is **what it takes to** solve this problem.
好的視覺能力是這個問題的解決之道。

191

情境對話   MP3 133

· Mom 媽媽
· Jack 傑克

M: Jack, I'm making your favorite flourless chocolate torte today. Can you do me a favor and chop up those chocolate chunks for me?

J: Any time. Chocolate torte is my one and only dessert. I can't imagine life without it!

M: If you know how to make it from scratch, you won't have to worry about that.

J: I'm putting the butter over simmering water for a water bath. But…mom, I think we run out of chocolate.

媽： 傑克，我今天要做你最愛的無粉巧克力蛋糕。可以請你幫個忙，把那些巧克力塊切碎嗎？

傑： 沒問題，巧克力蛋糕是我最喜歡的甜點，我無法想像沒有它的日子！

媽： 如果你知道如何從無到有做出蛋糕，那就不必擔心這個問題了。

傑： 我把奶油放在沸騰的水上隔水加熱，但…媽媽，巧克力好像沒了。

M: I knew it. That's why I bought another box right there in the cupboard.

J: You are a genius!

媽：我就知道，這就是我為什麼又買了一盒，就在碗櫥裡。

傑：妳是天才！

1 贏在起跑點——課堂知多少。

2 伴著孩子成長——親子教育。

Baking

延伸學習字彙

· dainty	小巧的
· melting	融化的
· silky	口感絲滑的
· buttery	奶油濃厚的
· flawless	完美無瑕的

Cake pan

常用烘焙器材

· sift	粉篩
· cake pan	蛋糕模
· spatula	橡皮刮刀
· rolling pin	麵棍
· mixing ball	攪拌盆
· hand-mixer	手提式打蛋器

 慣用語  MP3 134

from scratch 從頭開始

❶ John started making the bread **from scratch**.

約翰從零開始製作麵包。

❷ That restaurant makes everything **from scratch**, including mayonnaise.

那家餐廳的每樣東西都是自製的，包括美乃滋也是。

．．

any time 沒問題

❶ A: Thank you for giving me a hand.

B: **Any time**!

A：謝謝你的幫忙。

B：不客氣。

❷ A: Can you help me move the desk?

B: **Any time**.

A：可以幫我搬桌子嗎？

B：當然沒問題。

延伸句型  MP3 135

❶ one and only 最愛的

Chocolate torte is Jack's **one and only** love.
巧克力蛋糕是傑克的最愛。

❷ do someone a favor 幫忙

Jack **did his mom a favor** by helping her make a cake.
傑克幫媽媽做蛋糕，幫了媽媽一個忙。

❸ run out (of) 用完

The chocolate **ran out**. We need to buy another box.
巧克力吃完了，我們得再買一盒才行。

Festival
民俗節慶

・Dad 老爸
・Jack 傑克
・Mom 媽媽

D: Christmas is around the corner. You guys decide what to do yet?

J: The time has arrived! I'm busting Santa this year.

D: You can't do that! If you scare him away, there will be no gifts for you forever!

M: We can try some different decorations, some over-the-top ones.

D: And we can start a cookie baking contest indoor!

J: Guys, the holiday is not complete without a mug of hot

老：馬上就是聖誕節了，你們決定好要怎麼過了嗎？

傑：時候終於到了！今年我一定要逮到聖誕老人。

老：不行，如果你把他嚇跑的話，以後就再也收不到禮物了。

媽：我們可以來一點不同的裝飾，誇張些更好。

老：還可以舉辦室內餅乾烘焙大賽！

傑：各位，聖誕節沒有一杯熱可可就不完

cocoa. I would die for a mug with marshmallow right now!

整了。現在我超級想要來一杯裝滿棉花糖的熱可可！

1 贏在起跑點 —— 課堂知多少。

2 伴著孩子成長 —— 親子教育。

延伸學習字彙

Festive

- lively　　　　熱鬧的
- festive　　　　歡樂的
- convivial　　　和樂的
- thrilling　　　令人興奮的
- anticipated　　萬眾矚目的

認識節慶

Mid-Autumn Festival

- Dragon Boat Festival　端午節
- Mid-Autumn Festival　中秋節
- Halloween　　萬聖節
- Thanksgiving　感恩節
- Christmas　　聖誕節

the time has arrived 時候到了

❶ The time has arrived for Gina to learn about her weight.

時候到了，吉娜的體重數字即將揭曉。

❷ The time has arrived. I hope you are number one.

終於來到這一刻了，我希望你勇奪第一。

....

busted 逮到了

❶ Gina was **busted** eating doughnut in the bathroom.

吉娜被抓到在廁所裡吃甜甜圈。

❷ Jack said he would practice roller skating. However, he was **busted** playing video games at his friend's house.

傑克說他會去練滑輪。然而，他卻被逮到在朋友家打電動。

 延伸句型　MP3 138

❶ scare away 嚇跑

The little deer was **scared away** by the tiger.
老虎把小鹿嚇跑了。

❷ not complete without… 一定要有

Christmas is **not complete without** a Christmas tree.
聖誕節沒了聖誕樹就不完整了。

❸ to die for 極想要的，渴望

I'm **dying for** a piece of pizza.
我超想吃一片披薩。

1 贏在起跑點 —— 課堂知多少。

2 伴著孩子成長 —— 親子教育。

Unit 47

Diet
飲食習慣

 情境對話　 MP3 139

- Mom 媽媽
- Dolly 朵莉
- Jack 傑克

D: Mom, why are our plates loaded with vegetables? Why can't we eat meat?

M: Because we are practicing to have a vegetarian diet. We can take in egg and milk, but no meat.

J: I'm tired of eating carrots. Can I have steak and milkshake instead?

M: You will get used to this diet. It is said that having less red meat and more leafy greens will do good for your body.

J: I already had tons of kale.

朵：媽媽，為什麼我們的盤子裡都是蔬菜？為什麼我們不能吃肉？

媽：因為我們在練習吃素。我們可以攝取雞蛋和牛奶，但不能吃肉。

傑：我不想再吃紅蘿蔔了，可用牛排和奶昔替代嗎？

媽：你會習慣的。聽說少吃紅肉，多攝取綠葉蔬菜對你的健康有益。

傑：我已經吃好多的芥藍菜了。

M: Hmm, I guess maybe some chicken nuggets couldn't hurt.

媽：我想也許來點雞塊也無傷大雅。

1
贏在起跑點——
課堂知多少。

2
伴著孩子成長——
親子教育。

延伸學習字彙

Diet

· lean	精瘦的
· ideal	理想的
· dietary	飲食的
· habitual	慣性的
· genetic	基因的
· balanced	均衡的

各種飲食習慣

Gluten-free

· vegetarian	蛋奶素
· vegan	純素
· paleo	原始人飲食
· kosher	猶太飲食
· halal	清真飲食
· gluten-free	無麩質飲食

it is said that 聽說

❶ It is said that having less fried foods will reduce the risk of having cancer.

聽說少攝取油炸食品能降低罹患癌症的風險。

❷ It is said that one cup of coffee per day is good for the heart.

聽說每天來一杯咖啡對心臟有益。

. . . .

tons of 許多

❶ Each time Jack makes mistakes, he always has **tons of** excuses.

每次傑克犯錯，他總有說不完的藉口。

❷ There are **tons of** harvested crops in the barn.

穀倉裡有許多收成的穀物。

延伸句型　　MP3 141

❶ Loaded with 裝滿；載滿

The sleigh is **loaded with** logs.
雪橇上載滿木柴。

❷ Be tired of 對⋯感到厭倦

Santa **is tired of** traveling around the world every year.
聖誕老人對每年環遊世界感到疲累。

❸ Get used to 習慣於

Kelly has **got used to** the fast tempo in the city.
凱莉已經習慣都市的快速節奏。

Talking on the phone
電話用語

 情境對話　 MP3 142

- Peter 彼得
- Jack 傑克
- John 約翰

P: Hello. I'd like to speak to John, please.

J: Please hold the line.

J: Hi, this is John speaking.

P: Hi, it's me! Haven't heard from you for ages, how have you been?

J: I'm sorry, who is this? Can you speak up?

P: It's me! Peter! I want to talk about our coming fishing plan!

J: I believe you have the wrong number, sir.

彼：你好，請找約翰。

傑：請稍等。

約：你好，我是約翰。

彼：是我啦！好久沒你的消息了，你好嗎？

約：抱歉，你是哪位？可以請你大聲一點嗎？

彼：是我彼得啦！我想跟你聊聊之後的釣魚活動！

約：先生，我想你打錯電話了。

1 贏在起跑點 —— 課堂知多少。

2 伴著孩子成長 —— 親子教育。

Dial a number

延伸學習字彙

· available	有空的
· occupied	忙線中
· portable	可攜式的
· disposable	拋棄式的
· international	國際的
· long-distance	長途的

Leave a message

常用電話用語

· hold	暫留
· record	錄音
· transfer	轉接
· call back	回撥
· dial a number	撥號
· leave a message	留言

 慣用語  MP3 143

I'd like to 我想…

❶ I'd like to speak to Mary, please.
我想找瑪莉,謝謝。

❷ I'd like to have a medium-rare steak.
我想要一份五分熟牛排。

....

hold the line 請稍等(電話用語)

❶ Please **hold the line**. I'll pass through for you.
請稍等,我幫你接通。

❷ Would you please **hold the line**? Jason will be on the phone soon.
請你稍等一下,傑森立刻就來接聽了。

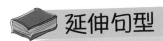 延伸句型　 MP3 144

❶ Speak up 大聲點

Please **speak up**. I have no idea what you are talking about.

請大聲點。我完全不知道你在説什麼。

······

❷ Talk about 談論

They are **talking about** going out after work.

他們在討論下班後出外走走。

······

❸ Have the wrong number 打錯電話

The guy who called for Judy **had the wrong number**. There is no Judy here.

打來找茱蒂的傢伙搞錯號碼了。這裡沒有茱蒂這個人。

情境對話　 MP3 145　· Dad 老爸
· Jack 傑克

J: Dad, is that iPhone X? I thought Mom forbad you to buy it.

D: My hard work finally paid off. Your mom has seen my efforts and permitted me to have this all-new device.

J: Cool! This is by far the best and the most expensive smartphone ever existed!

D: Totally worth every penny. Aside from great performance, its high-tech system and upgraded user experience is undebatable.

傑：老爸，那是 iPhone X 嗎？我以為媽媽不准你買下手。

老：我的努力終於有回報了。你媽媽看到我勤奮的模樣，才允許我買下這支全新上市的手機。

傑：酷！這是至今為止功能最強、也是最貴的智慧型手機耶！

老：每分錢都花得值得。除了強大的性能不說，高科技系統和更優質的使用者體驗，都是無可匹敵的。

J: Dad, do you think I can take over your iPhone 7?

D: No way! You're way too young!

傑：老爸，我能接收你的 iPhone 7 嗎？

老：不行，你還太小了。

Wireless earphones

延伸學習字彙

· digital	電子的
· advanced	先進的
· up-to-date	跟上潮流的
· sophisticated	精密的
· technical	技術性的
· high-tech	高端技術的

Speaker

常見 3C 裝置

· tablet	平板
· speaker	喇叭
· smartphone	智慧型手機
· wearable device	
穿戴裝置	
· personal computer	
個人電腦	
· wireless earphones	
無線耳機	

pay off 有了回報

❶ Jack has been studying hard and his hard work **paid off**. He got all A's this semester.

傑克一直都很用功念書，他的努力有了回報；這學期每個項目他都拿了甲上。

❷ My dad's determination **paid off**. He was promoted to general manager.

我老爸的決心終於有了回報，他被拔擢成總經理了。

by far 到目前為止

❶ Jack is **by far** the most hard-working student I've ever seen.

傑克是到目前為止我見過最認真向學的學生。

❷ **By far**, he has not made any mistakes.

到目前為止，他還沒犯過任何失誤。

 延伸句型 ● MP3 147

❶ aside from 除了…以外（還有）

Aside from chicken wings, the combo consists of two beef burgers.

除了雞翅以外，套餐還包含了兩個牛肉漢堡。

....

❷ worth + N. 值得

The combo is not **worth the money**.

套餐內容根本不值它的價錢。

....

❸ take over 接管

The boss decides to fire the manager and **take over** the business.

老闆決定開除經理，自己接管生意。

Watching news on TV
看新聞

 情境對話　 MP3 148

- Mom 媽媽
- Dolly 朵莉
- Jack 傑克

M: Look at that. The typhoon strikes South-East islands and people are freaking out.

媽：快看。颱風侵襲東南亞島嶼，人們都嚇壞了。

D: Mommy, I'm afraid of getting hit by a typhoon, too.

朵：媽媽，我怕颱風也會影響到我們。

M: It's okay, honey. Look, I've changed to another channel. These people are angry about the government.

媽：甜心，別怕。看，我轉到別的頻道了。這些人對政府感到很生氣。

D: Why are they angry?

朵：為什麼他們要生氣？

M: Due to the change in legislation, they have fewer day-offs now.

媽：因為立法改變的關係，他們現在的休假變少了。

J: I hope we live a low-profile life so that no one wants to disrupt us.

傑：希望我們生活低調，這樣就沒有人會來干擾我們了。

1 贏在起跑點——
課堂知多少。

2 伴著孩子成長——
親子教育。

News anchor

延伸學習字彙

· absurd	荒唐的
· exclusive	獨家的
· touching	感人的
· accidental	出人意表的
· disturbing	令人不安的
· nerve-racking	令人緊張的

Cameraman

常用新聞詞彙

· reporter	記者
· news anchor	主播
· cameraman	攝影師
· breaking news	突發新聞
· exclusive news	獨家報導
· headline news	頭條新聞

 慣用語  MP3 149

freak out 驚慌失措

❶ Jack lost his skates, so he was **freaking out**.
傑克把滑輪鞋弄丟,所以他簡直快急死了。

❷ Dolly couldn't find her doll. She **freaked out**.
朵莉找不到娃娃,她不知道該怎麼辦才好。

low-profile 低調的

❶ Jenny lives a **low-profile** life. Her colleges barely notice her.
珍妮的生活很低調。她的同事幾乎不會注意到她。

❷ This shirt has a **low-profile** but fashionable design.
這件上衣設計低調時尚。

  MP3 150

❶ be afraid of 擔心

Dolly **is afraid of** darkness.
朵莉很怕黑。

❷ angry about 對…感到憤怒

Don't be **angry about** her. It's not her fault.
別生她的氣，不是她的錯。

❸ due to 由於

Due to the exam, all students are not allowed to go in the second building until noon.
由於考試的緣故，所有學生中午以前都不能進入第二大樓。

1 贏在起跑點——課堂知多少。

2 伴著孩子成長——親子教育。

215

Reading magazines
讀雜誌

 情境對話 MP3 151

- Mom 媽媽
- Dolly 朵莉

M: Is that the latest Teen Vogue?

媽：那是最新一期的
《Teen Vogue》
嗎？

D: Yeah. It's a magazine that features celebrity fun stuff.

朵：對，這是一本專講
明星趣聞的雜誌。

M: I know what it is. I mean, why are you reading it?

媽：我知道，我是說，
妳怎麼會讀這本雜
誌？

D: Generally speaking, I read it twice a week, including Sunday.

朵：一般來講，我每個
禮拜會讀兩次，包
括星期日。

M: Honey, you are too young for this. Do you even know what Vogue means?

媽：甜心，妳太年輕
了，不該讀這個。
妳還知道 Vogue
是什麼意思嗎？

D: It refers to fashion. Believe it or not, mom, I'm learning a lot

朵：意思是時尚。媽
媽，信不信由妳，

from this magazine.

我從這本雜誌學到了不少的知識。

Magazine

延伸學習字彙

· timely	即時的
· thorough	透徹的
· specialized	專門的
· vague	模稜兩可的
· controversial	爭議性的
· eye-catching	吸引人目光的

Eye-catching

常用雜誌詞彙

· periodical	期刊
· quarterly	季刊
· rumor	謠言
· gossip	八卦
· scandal	醜聞
· love affair	花邊新聞

feature 以…為賣點

❶ These pants **feature** premium ventilation and sweat-wicking technology.

這些運動褲的特色是具有優良的透氣性以及排汗技術。

❷ The car **features** wide seats and a large compartment in the back.

這輛車的賣點是座位寬敞和大的後車廂。

....

believe it or not 信不信由你

❶ Believe it or not, these pants are as light as air.

信不信由你，這件運動褲輕盈得像空氣一樣。

❷ Believe it or not, I ate a whole pizza for breakfast.

信不信由你，我早餐吃了一整個披薩。

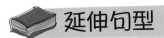 延伸句型  MP3 153

❶ generally speaking 一般而言

Generally speaking, ants move in bulk.
一般而言，螞蟻會集體行動。

❷ including⋯ 包括

There are three members in my family, **including** my dad, my mom, and I.
我家有三名成員，包括我爸爸、我媽媽和我。

❸ refer to 意指

Roses usually **refer to** love.
玫瑰通常代表愛情。

Unit 52

Snack
零食

 情境對話　 MP3 154　・Dad 老爸
・Jack 傑克

J: I catch you snacking again. Didn't you promise to swap potato chips for celery stalks?

傑：我又抓到你偷吃零食了，你不是答應過要把洋芋片換成芹菜莖嗎？

D: Yeah…In theory, I should be cutting down on sugar intake.

老：對啦…理論上來說，我應該減少攝取糖分的。

J: Just focus on the six-packs! You can do this!

傑：就專心想六塊肌！你辦得到的！

D: I know. But I really crave for these chips. They are so yummy…

老：我知道。但我真的很想吃洋芋片，洋芋片這麼好吃…。

J: It doesn't have to be this way, dad. Let's make some chips ourselves and eat healthier!

傑：老爸，你不必這麼辛苦。我們來自製洋芋片，吃得更健康一點吧！

D: What a good son I have!

老：我的兒子真好啊！

Popcorn

延伸學習字彙

· sweet	香甜的
· crunchy	酥脆的
· creamy	濃郁的
· handy	方便的
· snacky	嘴饞的
· hooking	令人上癮的

Mix nuts

常見零食

· wafer	威化餅
· mix nuts	綜合堅果
· popcorn	爆米花
· tortilla chip	墨西哥脆餅
· potato chip	洋芋片
· vegetable stick	蔬菜棒

慣用語  MP3 155

in theory 理論上來說

❶ **In theory**, this cake should be perfect after 30 minutes in the oven.

理論上來説，烤三十分鐘後，這個蛋糕就能完美出爐。

❷ **In theory**, with these two ingredients adding together, I'll be creating a perfect drink.

理論上來説，只要把這兩種原料加在一起，就能創造出完美飲料。

......

it doesn't have to be this way 無需如此

❶ Judy and Amy are having a cold fight, but **it doesn't have to be this way**.

茱蒂和艾咪在冷戰，但她們實在不必這樣。

❷ You're having a hard time staying up. **It doesn't have to be this way**.

你熬夜熬得很辛苦，真的不必這麼累。

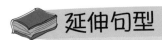  MP3 156

❶ swap A for B 以 B 取代 A

Dad decides to **swap burgers for salad**.
老爸決定把漢堡替換成沙拉。

....

❷ cut down on 減少

He is trying to **cut down on** carbohydrates.
他試著減少攝取碳水化合物。

....

❸ focus on 專注於

Focus on the goal and you will achieve it.
專注於目標，你總會成功的。

國家圖書館出版品預行編目(CIP)資料

我的第一本親子英語 / 陳怡歆、洪婉婷著.
-- 初版. -- 臺北市：倍斯特, 2018.4　面；
公分. --（文法生活英語系列；6）
ISBN 978-986-95288-9-4（平裝附光碟）
1.英語 2.學習方法 3.親子

805.1　　　　　　　　　　　107003888

文法/生活英語　006

我的第一本萬用親子英語（附學習光碟）

初　　版　　2018年4月
定　　價　　新台幣399元

作　　者　　陳怡歆、洪婉婷
出　　版　　倍斯特出版事業有限公司
發 行 人　　周瑞德
電　　話　　886-2-2351-2007
傳　　真　　886-2-2351-0887
地　　址　　100 台北市中正區福州街1號10樓之2
E - m a i l　　best.books.service@gmail.com
官　　網　　www.bestbookstw.com
執行總監　　齊心瑀
行銷經理　　楊景輝
執行編輯　　陳韋佑
封面構成　　高鍾琪
內頁構成　　菩薩蠻數位文化有限公司
印　　製　　大亞彩色印刷製版股份有限公司

港澳地區總經銷　　泛華發行代理有限公司
地　　址　　香港新界將軍澳工業邨駿昌街7號2樓
電　　話　　852-2798-2323
傳　　真　　852-2796-5471